A Lady's Curves

The Everton Domestic Society
Book 7

A.S. Fenichel

A Lady's Curves by A.S. Fenichel

All rights reserved.

Copyright © 2024 by A.S. Fenichel

No part of this book may be reproduced in any form or by any electronic or mechanical means, including information storage and retrieval systems, without written permission from the author, except for the use of brief quotations in a book review.

This book is a work of fiction and any resemblance to persons, living or dead, is purely coincidental. The characters are productions of the author's imagination. Locales are fictitious, and/or, are used fictitiously.

AI RESTRICTION: The author expressly prohibits any entity from using any part of this publication, including text and graphics, for purposes of training artificial intelligence (AI) technologies to generate text or graphics, including without limitation, technologies that are capable of generating works in the same style or genre as this publication.

The author reserves all rights to license uses of this work for generative AI training and development of machine learning language models.

Edited by Oopsie Daisy Edits

Cover design by The Swoonies Romance Art

Contents

A LADY'S CURVES	v
Chapter 1	1
Chapter 2	11
Chapter 3	19
Chapter 4	27
Chapter 5	35
Chapter 6	43
Chapter 7	51
Chapter 8	59
Chapter 9	67
Chapter 10	77
Chapter 11	85
Chapter 12	95
Epilogue	103
Also by A.S. Fenichel	107
About the Author	111

A Lady's Curves

Oscar Stafford, The Earl of Kendall, is in dire straits. While in Scotland avoiding the marriage mart, his steward ran off with one of the maids and quite a lot of money. Rather than cause a scandal, he hides the events that brought him back to London. If he obtains a new steward through the normal channels, all of the ton will know he was duped like a common fool. The Everton Domestic Society is renowned for being discreet, but can a woman do a man's job? Already full of doubts, one look at the beautiful and womanly form of Miss Ann Wittman, and Oscar's doubts are replaced by a rush of desire.

Ann Wittman has long been on the shelf. After three failed seasons, she joined the Everton Domestic Society to relieve her parents of their burden and make her way in the world. That was seven years ago. She's spent much of her employment helping other young ladies find appropriate matches—the worst punishment for not being a diamond of the first water. The opportunity to run estates rather than teach etiquette is too delicious to turn down. Oscar Stafford is far more stunning than any Greek statue, but his homes are in complete chaos. Ann will have to push aside a lifetime of pent-up desire if she's going to succeed in a man's world. Can she ignore the earl's allure and get the job done?

Chapter One

Ann

The front parlor of Everton House is quiet as I pull my embroidery needle through the cloth held in a wooden frame. The bluebirds will look lovely on a pillow and will make a nice gift for Lady Chervil. Admitting to boredom is not in my nature, so I stifle a sigh.

The parlor door opens and Lady Jane stands in the threshold. She is tall and her brown hair has begun to show a few strands of gray on the sides. "Miss Wittman, do you have a moment? There's a client in my office, whom I'd like for you to meet."

A short silent word of prayer for being saved from the doldrums, and I stand, leaving my needlework on the settee. "Of course, my lady. Do I need to change?" I look down at my dull blue day dress and brush out the skirt.

Jane smiles warmly. "You look very nice. No need to change."

Joining her in the doorway, I ask, "Who is the client?"

"The Earl of Kendall. He requires someone to replace his steward temporarily."

It's a short walk across the foyer to the office, so there's no time for more questions.

When the footman opens the office door, the man sitting on the sofa stands. He's very tall and broad. If not for the expensive clothes, he looks more like a blacksmith than an earl. His expression is sour, but his eyes are kind.

Jane says, "This is Miss Ann Wittman. Ann, may I introduce Oscar Stafford, the Earl of Kendall?"

He bows and I make a deep curtsy. "My lord, it's a pleasure to make your acquaintance."

"Miss Wittman." He clears his throat and stares over my shoulder. "Perhaps this was a bad idea. I can't see how a woman will be able to accomplish what I require."

Tempted to check and see if someone is standing behind me, I chalk his lack of direct gaze up to arrogance, something I've dealt with all my life. The earl is no exception. "I'm certain that whatever you need will not exceed my abilities. Lady Everton briefly told me that you require a steward. May I ask what happened to the last person who held the position?" Sitting across from him on an overstuffed chair, I feel uncertain and keep myself at the edge of the seat, should escape be necessary. It's silly really. Lady Jane is here and the footman is right outside the door. Yet, old habits are difficult to change.

Oscar sits with an audible sigh. "I didn't mean to offend you, Miss Wittman. I'm sure you are quite capable. The issue is that the position of the steward is a traditionally male role and I find myself at the Everton Domestic Society because all other options are not..." he pauses, his lips pulled in a straight line, "desirous at this time. My steward, who I hired a year ago after the previous one retired, left suddenly to marry one of the maids. I'm told they have taken up residence with her family in

Surrey. I have a house in London, a hunting lodge in Scotland, and a large estate in Devonshire. It is a big job to keep the accounts of all three properties." His gaze shifts uncomfortably.

It's strange for an employee to run off on short notice and the earl's demeanor is awkward, as if he might be lying. My suspicious nature awakens, but I keep my thoughts to myself. "What is the state of the bookkeeping, if I may ask, my lord?"

"I'm afraid, I was negligent in keeping tabs on things for some time. Mr. Bellston, the former steward, has left things untidy. I tried to sort it out, but find I need help." He meets my gaze for the first time since I entered the room.

Jane's expression remains calm and positive, as it always does. She smooths her perfectly ordered hair. "Miss Wittman has the required skills to help you. She has long been the society's lady in waiting, as she excels at helping young women move on to the next stage of their lives. However, this is not out of her comfort level and she has assisted me with Lord Everton's and my estates for many years."

"You are a nanny?" Oscar has no issue making eye contact now.

Never one to show temper, I stuff the roiling in my gut down. "I am an Everton Lady. I have held many positions over the last seven years."

He stands. "This will not work. I apologize for taking up your time, ladies."

Jane gets up, so I follow. Why would an earl come to the society for this post when there are more traditional ways of finding a new steward? "Lord Kendall, if it is discretion you're after, I am your best option."

His jaw ticks and he narrows his green eyes. "Even if that were true, how would I explain you to the ton? A woman of your age in my home, traveling with me to my country estates, it would be scandalous."

"I see your point, my lord," Jane says. "While I could send Miss Wittman with a chaperon, I doubt that would help. The gossip would be that you somehow lost your steward and hired a woman. People would meddle into what happened with Mr. Bellston, and I'm guessing you wouldn't want that." Without noticing Oscar's cringe, she continues, "I beg your pardon, Miss Wittman, but you're too old to be placed as the earl's ward. Besides, some people will remember your time out in society."

Wishing I could keep my cheeks from showing my embarrassment, I hold myself expressionless and nod.

"Do you have a niece or younger sister, my lord?" Jane taps her chin with her index finger.

"I don't know where you're going with this line of questioning, Lady Everton." His hands go to his hips and he strikes an imposing figure.

A soft smile pulls at Jane's lips. "Forgive me, I have an idea that would work if you have a young lady in your family whom you might take on as a ward. Then the world might be told that Miss Wittman is a governess and she could be in your homes without anyone questioning her presence."

My pulse races, and I can't decide if it's because of the notion of running such a large estate, the lies that will have to be told, or if there's a thrill at working with the man hovering over them. "I'm not an adept liar, Lady Jane."

Jane frowns.

Oscar grins. It's the first sign that he's more than a grumpy earl who lost control of his birthright. "I have a niece, Louisa, who is reluctant to make her appearance in society. My sister recently wrote me detailing her woes. Perhaps you wouldn't have to lie, Miss Wittman. If I sponsor Louisa, you could be her governess and also help me with my books." He pauses and frowns, then looks me in the eyes again. "But perhaps I ask too much."

"That would be acceptable, my lord." The flutter in my stomach returns when he stares at me, but I foist away any ridiculous emotions.

***

A week later, the carriage takes me across Mayfair for my new assignment with the Earl of Kendall and his niece Louisa.

The house fills one side of the square and has flowers growing in perfect rows out front. From the outside, everything looks perfect. I imagine that's the way Oscar Stafford likes everything.

My carriage stops in front of the gate and the Everton footman who accompanied me hands me down. "Thank you, Will."

Once across the courtyard, I bang the knocker.

A young maid of perhaps seventeen pulls the door open. "Are you Miss Wittman?"

"I am."

"You better come in." She leaves the door open and runs down a hall to the left of the foyer.

Blinking, I stare after her.

Will chuckles. "Seems you've got your work cut out for you, Miss Ann."

"It would seem so. Would you mind bringing my trunk around and make sure it gets in the house, Will?"

Giving me a serious look, he nods. "Of course. I'll see to it."

At least the foyer looks well-appointed. I step inside and close the door. Removing my bonnet and gloves, I place them on the half table to the left. A large chandelier, covered in cobwebs, hangs above two swooping staircases that rise to an elaborate landing. Aside from the dust, it looks in good condition.

Following the path of the maid who opened the door, I watch from the threshold of a front parlor where the earl is deep in an argument with a woman who shares many of his features. She is perhaps a few years younger than him and of strong voice.

"Mae, I only want to give Louisa a season where she might find a suitable husband. Is that so terrible? You wrote to me in despair that she would end a spinster." Oscar's voice is even, but there's frustration in the tight line of his lips.

It takes all of my training not to gasp at how the word spinster is said as if it were a terrible disease.

"You'll try to turn her into a hermit, and I won't have it, Oscar. I love you, but you are not a good role model for a young, impressionable girl. All you have ever done is lock yourself away in that old hunting lodge of Papa's and work on projects only you understand." Mae wraps her arms around herself. She's wearing a light coat despite the fine weather and hasn't removed her hat or gloves, clearly not intending to stay long.

In the corner, a young woman of perhaps sixteen sits on the bench by the pianoforte and strokes the keys without producing any notes. It seems as if there's a tune there, but she knows better than to play while her elders are arguing.

"I'm not going to go to Scotland during the season, Mae. I'm going to stay here and clean up the mess. I have an Everton Lady coming for Louisa." He touches the mantle, then rubs his fingers together with a frown.

No doubt the parlor is as dusty as the foyer.

Clearing my throat, I cross the threshold. "Perhaps I may be of assistance."

"Ah. Excellent timing." Oscar rushes over and bows. "Miss Wittman, will you tell my sister that you shall not allow her daughter to become a hermit or pick up any of my other abhorrent habits?"

It's difficult not to laugh. "I shall do my best, but having no knowledge of your behavior, I'll reserve my promises." I cross to Mae and make a curtsy. "How do you do? I'm Ann Wittman from the Everton Domestic Society."

"Lady Mae Bartholomew, Countess of Creeves. I have always heard fine things about your society. My brother thinks you will help him hide his misfortunes from the ton while also helping my daughter find a husband of worth."

Louisa has dark hair, keeps her head down, and her attention on whatever music is in her head. She's lovely.

"I will help him sort out his accounts. Your daughter is a beautiful young lady. It shouldn't be difficult to find a fine gentleman to offer for her if that's what she wishes."

Mae snorts and it's extremely unladylike. "My daughter would be happy to sit in a music room and never come out. Can you cure that, Miss Wittman?"

Looking up, Louisa's eyes widen, and her hand stills.

It can't have been easy growing up, expected to stay in the open when you want to be in hiding. I smile in hopes of reassuring Louisa. "Perhaps there's no need for a cure, just a gentleman willing to sit and listen or even sing along."

The sun catches a glisten of emotion in Louisa's eyes. Her expression eases, but she keeps her attention on me.

A long moment passes when Mae studies me. It's a bit like being the fish in the bowl. She stares until most people would be uncomfortable, but I smile and wait.

With a nod, Mae says, "Fine. You may have your niece for the one season, Oscar, but only because I think Miss Wittman will be good for her. Perhaps she'll be good for you as well. This entire mess may be just the thing to force you out of your studies and into life. You have responsibilities to your title."

"I'm aware." He looks like a man who wants to leave the room, but knows how rude that would be, and that he'd lose the battle he's nearly won.

"Louisa, come and hug me so I can get out of this dusty attic of a house."

Mother and daughter hug, and Mae says a curt goodbye before striding out. The last thing we hear is an exasperated, "No butler," before the front door opens and closes.

Oscar laughs and the sound is magical, as if the world has been waiting years for it. "One thing is certain, Miss Wittman, you are not easily intimidated. My sister is a champion at making people feel uncomfortable, but you faced her like a Valkyrie."

Hard as it is to keep from smiling, I bite my lip and stare at him. Why must he be so attractive and large? "Lady Creeves is protecting her child from you, my lord."

Louisa giggles.

"I don't know why. It seems to me everyone wins in our plan." He returns to his frown, which seems to be his resting state. A shame, as his smile is most appealing.

Running my fingers along the back of the settee, I clear a line in the dust. "Why is the house so dusty, where are your butler and housekeeper? I assume the maid who answered the door when I knocked holds neither of those roles."

"I think that was the scullery maid, Susie." He rubs the back of his neck and flops into a chair near the fireplace. Dust swirls around him and he sneezes.

I retreat to the piano bench and sit with Louisa, who has returned to that corner. Perhaps because it's not quite as filthy. "Will you answer my questions, my lord?"

He seems to find a spot on the rug more interesting than the people in the room with him, but he finally lifts his head and meets my gaze. "I think they may have left with Mr. Bellston.

Neither had been in my employ for very long. I pensioned the old butler and maid less than a year ago."

Things are coming into focus. "And Mr. Bellston hired their replacements?"

"He did." He returns his gaze to the floor.

"Very well." With a sigh that I fail to stifle, I rise and pull the cord for service.

Chapter Two

Oscar

I knew I was making a mistake before signing the contract with the Everton Domestic Society. One look at Ann Wittman's soulful gray eyes, full bosom, and luscious curves, and I should have walked, no run, out and never looked back.

The issue is that I need her help. That was the only reason I stayed and agreed to have her in my home. It wouldn't do to have the entire ton know that I was duped. They already think I'm an oddity who only loves the wilds of Scotland and the natural world.

In one day in residence, Ann had my study, the parlor, and three of the bedrooms thoroughly cleaned.

The maids are hard at work cleaning the rest of the house at Ann's command.

As if my thoughts conjured her, she knocks on the open door to my study. "May I enter, my lord?"

Heart pounding, I stand. "Of course, Miss Wittman." I

gesture to the chair, round my desk, and join her in the seating area. The room is so much cleaner, it's hardly recognizable.

"About the butler and housekeeper, do you know where they are?" She never takes her gaze from mine. "Oh, and are they in good health?"

"I told you, they went with Mr. Bellston. I think they're in Surry." Even that's only a guess.

Her smile muddles my senses. Smart and lovely, when she smiles, she's like the dawn of a new day. If I'm not careful, she'll turn me into a poet.

"I meant the former housekeeper and butler, whom you pensioned. Do you know where they are? Perhaps they'd be willing to return temporarily or for a longer term if they are up to it."

"I hadn't thought of that." Such a simple solution to what seemed insurmountable. She's smarter than I thought, smarter than me, for certain. Why does everything about this Everton lady intrigue me?

"If you'll give me their addresses, I'll write to them on your behalf and see if some arrangements can be made. I assume you're able to compensate them, as well as a few more maids and a lady's maid for the young miss." Ann continued her direct regard.

Some people are intimidated by my size and growly demeanor. Ann is not among them. As far as I can tell, my presence does not affect her at all and it's damned frustrating. "I am fully solvent. I know it seems as if I'm inept, but that's not entirely true."

Her hands are neatly folded in her lap. Her peach day dress hasn't a single wrinkle. She came with no lady's maid, so how is she always perfect? "What do you do in Scotland?"

"I beg your pardon?" How does she know about Scotland?

"Your sister lamented your time there and you also

mentioned it when we first met. I wondered what attracts you to that house so much that you neglected your other properties." There's no judgment in her questions, only curiosity.

"I enjoy the quiet of Bielddubh. I'm working on an experiment to see if blending crops can make them unpalatable for insects yet maintain the taste for humans to enjoy. I have many other scientific experiments ongoing there as well." This is the point where most people's eyes glaze over.

Ann's brighten. "That's fascinating. Did you make any progress?"

"Some. Though not as much as I'd hoped for." I keep it vague as I've learned that boring people with my theories only sends them away faster. For some reason, I don't want Ann to go away.

"I'd like to hear more about it, but perhaps you'd better show me the bookkeeping records for the houses. Do you have all three here?"

"I brought everything from Bielddubh, and of course, this house's records are available. I didn't have time to go to Kensfield Manor. We'll have to make a trip there at some point." I have arguments ready for her rebuke. I expect she'll refuse to travel with me out of London or run back to Everton House immediately.

Nodding, Ann smiles. "Let's have a look at what you have."

I go to the desk, and she follows. I pull two stacks of books and papers from the lower drawer and place them on the desk. "Would you like to work here? I can occupy myself elsewhere if you wish."

"That's fine, my lord. At some point, I may have questions." She sits in my father's chair, and I think it suits her better than it ever did me.

There's something about her that soothes me. My time in London has always felt rushed, as I wished to be anywhere else.

Suddenly, the family house doesn't feel as daunting as it has in the past.

Perhaps I should do what other men of my rank do and go to the gentleman's club. Or I could help in the gardens, which are the only part of this house still functioning as they should. Instead, I take a book from the shelf and sit near the hearth. Ann might have questions for me. I should be available to her.

Thirty minutes pass before I realize the book is about parliamentary law. As I have not filled my father's seat, it's not interesting. I should change my ways and be a better, more normal earl. The very thought makes me nauseous.

Head down, Ann turns page after page. She organizes and makes notes as I watch from the other side of the room.

When she looks up, she catches me staring at her. "You didn't mention that Mr. Bellston ran off with more than the maid, my lord. He appropriated quite a bit of your money as well."

It's not as if I thought she wouldn't find it. I just hoped she'd ignore it and move on. "It's irrelevant to the job I wish you to do, Miss Wittman."

She folds her forearms at the edge of the desk which pushes her breasts up to the point where I worry for the ability of her frock to contain them.

My discomfort grows, and I adjust my seat to ensure she can't detect my state.

After a moment, she cocks her head. "You don't intend to recover those funds or make the man pay for his crime against you?"

"No. That would mean all of England knowing he'd played me for a fool." My gut knots, but at least my arousal has faded.

"I suppose pride is an excuse for letting a thief get away with so much money, but it's not a good one. You leave this man out in society where he can hurt other unsuspecting people." Her cheeks get rosy, but her expression remains calm.

The longer I look at her, the more I wonder if this arrangement is a good idea. I could call Lady Jane Everton and tell her that as bright as Miss Wittman is, she cannot come to my house. Last night I drank enough to fall asleep and not think of her down the hall. I can't behave like that every night. Perhaps if she were disdainful toward me, my desire would wane. "I shall let those other people deal with their own problems. It is not my function to rescue the world."

Her adorable chin wrinkles before she returns her attention to the pages on the desk. "Your point is taken, my lord."

"Once we've hired a proper lady's maid for Louisa, I think it would be better if you lived at Everton House and worked here as needed. I'm sure that would be more suitable for you as well as for me. Having a stranger in the house all the time isn't advisable in this day of shysters and thieves." As soon as the words are out of my mouth, I wish them back in.

As if the world has slowed, Ann closes the account book and lifts her gaze to mine. "Perhaps you are right. It will be strange to have a governess who doesn't live in your home, but I shall think of something to explain that away should anyone ask."

The eyes that I admired for the last hour have turned cold. She despises me and I deserve it. I wanted this and I can see that I'm getting exactly what I asked for. So, why does my chest ache as if someone even larger than me threw a bag of grain on top of it? I should be happy. If she hates me, all temptation is removed.

I've never been more miserable in my life. "I'm certain you will conjure a believable story."

Her jaw shifts from side to side before she stands. Never taking her attention from me, she walks to the door. "I don't know how I offended you, my lord. I think that this arrangement is in error. I am neither a thief nor a liar. I agreed to this at your request and with the understanding that you would behave as a gentleman. Had I known that you would be insulting, I would have remained in the Everton parlor, bored out of my mind."

My upbringing forces me to my feet when she rises. It takes all my energy to stay near the fireplace. My short nails dig into my palms as punishment for my abhorrent behavior. I remain in place as she turns on her heels and leaves the study.

I'm still frozen a moment later when Louisa walks in. "Uncle, what is wrong with Miss Wittman?"

"Nothing. Why do you ask?" I return to my seat and pick up the law book, which I have no intention of reading.

"She ran up the stairs and ignored my greeting. I think she may have been crying. Did you say something to upset her? She hardly seems the type to fall to tears easily. After all, she withstood my mama." She turns and looks toward the foyer and stairs. "Perhaps I should go check on her."

My soul is straining with pain. I'm a terrible person. I hurt a lovely woman to quell my own feelings. In the end, none of that has changed and I'm no longer a gentleman. "Louisa, you can go practice your pianoforte. I shall check on Miss Wittman. It was my callousness that injured her."

"Uncle, what did you do?" Generally demure, she looks ready to do me physical harm with her fist clenched at her hips. "We need Miss Wittman to get me a suitable and not horrible husband so I don't have to go back and live with Mother after the season. Besides, she seems a very nice lady. Why would you hurt her feelings?"

"Because I'm a dolt." I put the book aside, stride from the study, and up the stairs. I have no idea what I'm going to say.

Soon I'm standing outside Ann's guest quarters and have

no idea how to make this right without giving away my ungentlemanly thoughts regarding her. I have made an impossible situation worse. I tap on her door. "Miss Wittman?"

There's no reply.

"Ann?" I lean on the door frame. "Forgive me. I'm an unmitigated ass. I know you are a fine lady of unquestionable morals and ethics."

The door swings open, nearly toppling me. Ann's eyes are red, as are her nose and cheeks. "They why would you imply otherwise, my lord." She narrows her gaze. "Or have we taken liberties and I'm to call you Oscar now?"

I like the sound of my name on her lips. I like it far too much. There is a solution. "Miss Wittman, I'm sorry. I must decline to explain my behavior downstairs. However, I do not wish for you to leave. Louisa needs you. I need you." Closing my eyes so she's not so beautiful and near helps me to gather my thoughts.

"I don't think I can stay in the same house with you, my lord. You have created an environment where I no longer feel safe." The last word is tight and holds back more emotions.

"I will leave. I can stay at my club or with my mother and you can stay here with Louisa. I will attend whatever balls you think will help her cause. If you require my attention on business issues, you may send a footman with a note and I will come." I swallow down regret and desire and hope this arrangement is enough. "I'm not above begging you, Ann. I made a promise to my sister not to mention my obligations to my title. I need you here, but my presence is beside the point." The irony is not lost on me. All these years, I wanted to be left alone. I wanted the Earl of Kendall to go unnoticed and now I've made myself extraneous.

With wide blue eyes, she backs up several steps. "This makes no sense."

"I know it seems that way," I say from the threshold. "I have ruined a great many things in my life. It has always been this way. Let me do this one thing right, at least for my niece."

She stares out the window for a long moment. "I will agree to this, but I hope you will explain your behavior at some point. For now, it's enough that you have apologized and will leave the house. I have one condition."

Heart in my throat, I say, "Yes?"

Turning, she has her emotions under control and only her swollen eyes and red nose betray that she had been crying. "I will contact Lady Jane and see if Lady Honoria Chervil can join me here. She will act as a chaperon and thus protect my reputation."

I can see where my erratic behavior has made her feel protection is required. "Of course, invite Lady Chervil to join you here and let Lady Everton know she can increase my invoice for service to accommodate a chaperon."

She folds her hands together in front and nods. "Very well. I will stay. I will let you know when we are ready to begin accepting invitations."

"Thank you." I step back. "I'll pack and be out of the house within the hour."

She frowns. "Do you not have a valet, my lord?"

"I've never seen the point. I can take care of myself." The truth is that I never took the time to hire one. The valet from my youth was elderly and died when I was sixteen. My father died a few years later. Living in Scotland focused on science; having a valet never seemed important.

Even when she rolls her eyes, Ann is beautiful. "I shall put a valet on my list of employees to hire."

I force a serious look even though I want to smile. With a bow, I turn and go to my chamber to pack and leave the house.

Chapter Three

Ann

Lady Honoria Chervil sweeps into the study in a pink day dress and with a warm smile. "This is a fine house. Why is there no butler?"

"That is one of many good questions." I'm always filled with warmth when Lady Honoria is present. She's what the Evertons call a dowager. She never takes on assignments for herself, but she chaperons and is a great source of wisdom.

"Lady Jane told me that his lordship has left the residence." She sits on the chair near the hearth. "This is a cozy room."

I suppose it is. "His lordship is a moody sort. He's gone to stay at his club. At least, that's what the note he sent this morning said. I have written to the pensioned butler and housekeeper who preceded those who abandoned the house. It seems they are a married couple who the earl pensioned ten months ago. The recently hired steward replaced them for his scheme. The three thieves left together about a month ago with one of the maids. The earl wishes our discretion concerning the funds removed from the estate's accounts."

Shaking her head, Honoria sighs. "Proud man."

"Indeed." It's been a full day since I've seen Oscar Stafford, but my attraction for him hasn't waned any more than my rage toward him. It's a mystery to me how those two things can exist within me regarding the same person. "With Lady Jane's help, I have lined up a few interviews this afternoon. We must find two footmen, a downstairs maid, and a lady's maid for Miss Bartholomew."

"That is quite a lot to accomplish, but we can manage." Honoria is always optimistic. It's one of the things I love about her.

Carriage wheels sound out front.

I rise to answer the door, but as I arrive in the foyer, the door swings open. A gray-haired man dressed impeccably as a butler with a black coat and perfectly tied cravat steps in and narrows his gaze at the house. When he looks at me, he asks, "Are you Miss Wittman?"

Closing the distance, I curtsy. "Miss Ann Wittman."

He bows. "Theodore Jenkin. You may call me Jenkin." He turns and takes the hand of a woman in a dark-blue day dress. "This is my wife, Pamela Jenkin. We are the former butler and housekeeper of this house. Your note was unexpected, Miss Wittman."

"That is an understatement." Mrs. Jenkin steps forward. "Has his lordship reconsidered pensioning us?"

I'm unable to discern if Mrs. Jenkin is joking. "His lordship is in need of your help as the staff who replaced you were inadequate and hence are no longer here." It's not exactly the entire truth, but not false either.

A wide grin pulls at Mrs. Jenkin's lips forcing her full cheeks to plump.

Mr. Jenkin frowns. "And are we to be compensated or is our pension meant to be our salary? For how long does his lordship intend to keep us on?" His heavy gray-and-black eyebrows pull together. "Who says that we want to go back to work? We don't owe the Earl of Kendall anything."

"No indeed." His wife fists her hands, then crosses them over her chest. "Tossed us out with only a day's notice. We've had to go and live with my sister. Imagine that after all our years of service."

It is an appalling way to have treated people in his employ. "If you will come into the study and sit down. I'll have tea brought up, and we can discuss the entire situation and your compensation going forward."

Mrs. Jenkin grins. "I like the sound of that. A far cry more polite than that Belliston chap who sent us packing."

Lady Chervil says, "You will find that when an Everton Lady is in the house, things become much more civilized. I am Lady Honoria Chervil and will be assisting Miss Wittman and Miss Bartholomew for the season."

We make our way as a group into the study. I pull the bell for tea, then sit in one of the chairs around the low table. "Please have a seat."

"Miss Bartholomew? Isn't that his lordship's niece?" Jenkin waits for all three ladies to sit before he does so with his back perfectly straight and his eyes narrowed on me.

"I haven't seen her since she was a child. What is she doing here?" Mrs. Jenkin's expression has softened since entering the house.

Unsure how much to explain, I say, "His lordship is sponsoring Louisa for her first season. I will assist in finding her a suitable match. I will also be helping with his three estates. The former steward left them in a bit of a mess and took with him the butler and housekeeper he'd hired, along with the downstairs maid."

"Erma? I never trusted that girl." Mrs. Jenkin huffs and grips the arm of the settee until her knuckles are white.

I feel the tide is turning in my favor. "As you can imagine, the remaining staff were without guidance and when I arrived, the dust was thick, making the home unlivable. I've given what instruction I can and the cleaning has been done, but we are woefully understaffed and I am neither a housekeeper nor a butler."

They both nod with serious expressions tugging their mouths into straight lines. Jenkin's chest puffs out and his shoulders go back farther.

"I was hoping you both might come back to work. I've been authorized to offer you a twenty percent increase in your salaries and when you are ready to retire, the pensions will be far more fitting to your station." I lower my eyes to the rust and beige rug and wait.

Jenkin huffs a big growly sound.

Mrs. Jenkin says, "For what we have been put through, Oscar Stafford can make it twenty-five percent and no tossing us out without proper notice." She points her finger at me.

Smiling on the inside, I give them each a serious look. "I can agree to twenty-five percent and no one will be tossing you anywhere. I have his lordship's word that you will be able to work here until you are ready to leave, and at that time, the estate will take far better care of you."

They look at each other and some silent agreement is made before Mr. Jenkin stands and offers his hand. "We accept. We can come back tomorrow with our things and be ready to get to work."

Practically jumping for joy, I leap up and shake his hand. "I'm so pleased. I will have the Kendall carriage drive you back and it will return for you in the morning. No need to hire another hack."

"Everton Domestic Society, you say." The butler gives me a long look.

"Yes, Jenkin. We are ladies who have chosen honest work in the service of others, though our employment is generally for the short term. Once I've sorted out the books and houses, I'll hire a reputable steward and move on to another assignment." I have no idea why that should create an ache in my chest. I should be happy with the idea of not seeing Oscar again. His behavior is erratic and socially inappropriate. Still, there were moments when he looked at me and my heart pounded in a way that was different than the effect anyone else has ever had.

I brush that silliness aside and see the Jenkins to the door.

Closing it behind them, I lean on the inside.

Honoria grins at me. "I'm surprised they didn't ask after the earl."

"He prefers the house in Scotland. I think they rarely saw him."

"A shame he's so difficult, but I know you'll sort him, his niece, and his estates out. You're the finest of all the Everton Ladies." Honoria sways and climbs the steps. It's as if there is music only she hears.

I think she exaggerates. I'm just the only one who continues on at Everton. Many ladies come for a season or two and find husbands, or return home. For me, Everton House is home. So why does that make me sad?

I've moved my work to the small lady's desk near the bookshelves. It's the opposite side of the study which is at least thirty feet long and fifteen feet wide. This way I can leave notes on papers that I need Oscar to sign or read over, but he and I are not sharing the same space.

It's been a week since he moved out.

The household has accepted its first invitation to a ball tomorrow night. I feel more nervous than Louisa.

"That was my mother's desk. I offered to give it to her when she moved to the dower house, but she declined, saying that she wanted new things for her new start." Oscar stands in the doorway to the study with his hands behind his back.

I rise and curtsy.

He bows. His expression looks pained, with creases at the outer corners of his eyes and his lips pulled into a frown. He's in evening clothes, but nothing fancy, just a black evening suit and a white shirt with a cravat.

"I was not expecting to see you until tomorrow, my lord." I'm gripping the edge of the desk as if it's holding me across the room.

Stepping inside, he leans on the back of his desk. "I apologize. I should have sent a note. It seems the valet, Bolton, who you sent to me needs access to my full wardrobe if I'm to be presentable at a ball. I came along to make sure that you have everything you need."

"Yes. We are fine. I'm glad Bolton is working out. He came highly recommended. I've also hired a new maid and lady's maid for Louisa." My voice sounds tentative. I don't like it. I pull my shoulders back and lift my chin to bolster my courage.

He smiles. "I saw Jenkin when I entered. He gave me a piece of his mind."

I'm about to defend the butler, but Oscar holds up a hand

to stop me. "He has every right to be cross with me. It was kind of him and Mrs. Jenkin to return."

"At a twenty-five percent increase to their wage." I can't help liking that they bargained for more money.

"I'm sure they were woefully underpaid and deserved the increase." He stares at his highly polished shoes before looking at me. "Does Louisa have what she needs for the ball?"

"Yes. Your sister sent her trunk. She has a very fine selection of gowns for the season." I have so many questions to discern his character, but I keep them to myself.

"And you?" His green eyes cut through me as if he can see into my soul.

Swallowing down the effects, a nervous giggle tries to escapes. I quash it. "What about me?"

"Do you have everything you need to attend a ball?" His voice is soft, warm, and filled with warning.

Those bells ring in my ears. "I will be appropriately dressed for my position, my lord."

He straightens and clears his throat. "Of course."

"May I ask you something?" I release the desk and step closer.

He nods, his gaze boring through me.

"If you knew your staff was underpaid, why did you do nothing to correct the situation?" One of the many questions floating in my mind.

Turning, he walks to the threshold and stops. I think he's going to ignore my question when he turns back and locks his gaze with mine. "That would have required leaving my comfortable hiding place and rejoining my life, Miss Wittman. I don't generally like to do that. I should have been born a simple farmer or a man of science, but fate is cruel and made me an earl."

"Perhaps Mr. Bellston did you a favor." I wish I could take it back the moment I've said it.

"You think I deserved to be cheated and for my estates to go neglected?" There's an edge to his voice that is at once intriguing and frightening.

Closing the gap between us, it feels as if my shoes are filled with stones. "No. Not that. Nor do I think your staff deserved their treatment. However, his actions did get you to leave Scotland and join your life, even if it was unwillingly."

Those beautiful green eyes darken and he lowers his gaze. "You have seen my disposition, Ann. Do you really think society has any place for me?"

Before I can formulate a response, he walks out and a moment later, the front door closes.

My problem is that I do think he has a place in society. I just can't figure out why I think so or what that place is.

Chapter Four

Oscar

I have not attended a ball since I was twenty-two and my mother forced a season on me. Once she realized I was hopeless, she let me stay home with my experiments. I remember the anxiousness caused by swarms of people and the mothers with young daughters of a marrying age. That familiar knot twists in my stomach as we enter the Markelson Ball.

Louisa's hand tightens around my arm. "Uncle, I may be sick."

It wouldn't do to tell her that I may join her, so I pat her hand. "You look beautiful and we shall get through this together."

Her large green eyes stare at me. "Do you really think so?"

I force a smile. "I do. One step at a time, my dear. You'll dance with a few gentlemen, Miss Wittman will make sure they act the part, and I will escort you home in a few hours."

Ann steps out from behind us and whispers, "You might

even try to enjoy the process. You like to dance. I know you like music. Have a good time." She gives me a hard look.

Looking terrified, Louisa releases my arm and strides to a group of ladies around her age.

"I thought my sister might make an appearance." I scan the room. "I don't see her. Perhaps she really does trust you. I'm certain she doesn't trust me."

"You might try giving her a reason to." Ann steps back so that she's partially hidden by a potted tree. The things are all over the room, creating privacy.

"Are you hiding?" I can't help frowning at the navy-blue gown that covers almost every inch of her and looks as if it should be worn by someone twice her age.

"What are you scowling at, and no. I'm keeping my place. I'm a servant, not a debutante." Somehow, she makes herself even smaller.

"You know, when you said you had appropriate clothes for a ball, I didn't expect you to wear some maiden aunt's frock. Though you can make anything look lovely." I long to touch her, but keep my hands clasped behind my back.

Lifting her shoulders, she cocks her head. "You just complimented me." She stares into the crowd. "Thank you. I gave away my party gowns long ago. What I have is suitable for my current position in life."

I wish I could hide under the tree, but I'm a brutishly large man and all I can do is draw attention to myself. Before I can ask why someone who, based on her educated language and manners, was raised in society, never found a husband, a familiar voice calls my name.

"Oscar. You look..." My mother stares a full two beats. "Undisheveled."

Leaning down, I kiss her cheek. "Hello, Mother. I have a valet. He is to blame for my tidy appearance."

Mother is tall and slender with slightly graying brown hair done up in an elaborate style with diamonds and emeralds wrapped around a bun at the top. She looks as regal as ever. "You hired a valet? I hope I don't sound condescending, Oscar, but I'm proud of you."

It's impossible not to laugh. I like that my mother is happy with me even though I cannot take the credit. "Miss Ann Wittman of the Everton Domestic Society is the one you should compliment." I gesture to Ann.

Ann steps out from her hiding place.

"Miss Wittman, my mother, the Dowager Countess of Kendall."

With a slow curtsy, Ann says, "A pleasure to meet you, my lady."

Mother studies Ann. "Everton Domestic Society? Are you not the daughter of Sir Niles Wittman?"

"I am." Ann's cheeks pinken, but she keeps her gaze direct.

Tapping her closed fan against her palm, Mother narrows her gaze. "You are assisting my son?"

"I hired—"

Mother puts up a palm, calling for my silence. "I asked Miss Wittman."

It's a complete surprise when Ann's lips pull up in a gentle smile. She folds her gloved hands together at her waist. "His lordship needed a temporary steward as well as someone to help with the season for your granddaughter. I have been hired for those purposes."

"Louisa is here?" She looks around the ballroom and when she sees Louisa talking to the Marquis of Barton, Mother's face transforms into a joyful smile. "Isn't she beautiful? However did you get her away from the pianoforte?"

In a soft voice for Mother's ears only, Ann says, "I told her there were men who also love music. I hope she'll find a match that will make her happy in whatever life she chooses."

Mother smiles with love shining in her eyes. "It's possible. I loved the previous Earl of Kendall very much."

Ann steps back as if again taking a servant's position.

I don't like it even though I know it is expected. I file the name of her father away to ask her about at some other time.

Mother snaps out of her expression of love for Louisa and faces Ann. "Do not turn her into an Everton Lady or whatever you call yourselves. You should have married while you had the chance. I'm old enough to remember your first season, Miss Ann Wittman, or should I say Lady Ann?"

While there is no change in Ann's mild expression, the fire goes out of her eyes. "I was hired to help the young lady find an advantageous and happy match. If that is possible, I will do exactly that."

Louisa ends the conversation by appearing and greeting her grandmother with affection. "I didn't know you would be here, Grandmama. Four gentlemen have signed my dance card." She's more excited about the prospect than I would have expected.

"How very good. Let me see who they are." Mother gushes over the card with Louisa.

The two cross to a group of ladies with their mothers.

I move to stand beside Ann. "I apologize for my mother. She is protective of Mae and her grandchildren."

"No need for an apology, my lord." She fidgets with her gloves. "Is your mother not protective of you as well?"

Is she? I give the idea some thought. "I believe she used to worry about me, but perhaps sees me as a lost cause now." I gaze across the room and find the object of our conversation staring back.

Mother's eyebrows rise and she studies Ann for a long

moment before the conversation with a stern-looking woman in a peach gown pulls her attention.

"What did she mean when she said you had the chance to marry?" It's none of my business, but I can't help myself.

With a sigh, Ann says, "It is a long and uninteresting story, my lord. Perhaps one day when we are very bored, I will regale you with the folly of my youth and you will share your past with me."

Part of me wants to sway her from knowing any of what I did in the past. However, I don't push the idea aside as I might normally. "I look forward to that day, Lady Ann." With a bow, I cross to see what Mother and Louisa are conspiring about. Mae will never forgive me if I let our mother have too much say in any part of her daughter's season.

An hour later, I'm watching Louisa dance with her second partner. He's a skinny young man with red hair and a long nose. I check the potted tree where Ann has been hiding for the entire night, only to find the space empty.

A tall blonde woman steps into my view. Her hair is elaborately curled on the top of her head and her bright blue eyes are very wide. She is admittedly very pretty. "Lord Kendall, you may not remember me."

Mind elsewhere, I attempt to focus on the woman; she does look familiar. "Forgive me, madam, I am at a loss."

Her smile brightens and it's easy to find her pleasing to look at. "When I was twelve, you saved me from a horse that had gone wild. I am Lady Rebbecca Dunbar." She curtsies.

I bow. "I do remember you. It was at your father's estate and the groom had put you on a horse not suitable for riding by anyone, let alone a child. I'm glad to see you are fully recovered from the incident."

"It was eight years ago, my lord. I never did recover from seeing you galloping across the field like a madman and sweeping me off of that horse. I was certain I would die that day." She shivers and it seems genuine to the memory of a very close call.

"It was my honor to come to your aid." I search the room for Ann before bringing my attention back to Rebbecca.

"Would you think me very forward if I asked you to dance the next with me?" She has lowered her voice and leaned in.

While I know the lady is flirting with me, I'm not as appalled by it as I have been in years past when ladies attempted to appeal to me in a search for a husband. She's pleasant and lovely. It can do no harm to have one dance with a pretty girl even if she or her mother will make more of it. "I would be honored, Lady Rebbecca."

The music begins again with the tapping of a conductor's wand and I have no time to consider the error of saying yes. Giving her my arm, I escort her to the floor and struggle to remember the steps of the quadrille.

It takes less time than I expected before it all comes back to me. I swirl Miss Dunbar around the dance floor in time with the music and even manage a brief conversation as the dance permits. At the edge of the room, I catch a glimpse of navy blue dashing from behind an orange tree and out the French doors to the garden. There is another ten minutes to the quadrille, but now my mind is on Ann and where she has gone.

Mother grins at me from the fireplace while she sips lemonade.

Keeping my face serene, I'm rolling my eyes on the inside.

Louisa is happily dancing with yet another dull-looking young man, but she looks happy enough.

When the music finally ends, I bow. "Thank you for the dance, Lady Rebbecca."

"It was a pleasure, Lord Kendall. If you should like to pay me a call, I would be happy to see you tomorrow." Gaze direct, she makes a curtsy and walks away.

I make my way to the door where I last saw Ann. The night air is a refreshing change from the hot, crowded ballroom. I step to the edge of the stone patio searching the torch-lit garden. My heart begins to beat faster and my chest tightens.

Making my way along the central path, I head in the direction of a central fountain. The sighs and moans of lovers making use of the shadows and tall shrubs stir feelings in me that I'm unfamiliar with. Does Ann have a lover? Is she meeting him here for a tryst? Jealousy that I have no right to swells within me.

As I reach the circular area around the fountain, I see her. She's not alone. "I'm warning you to unhand me, sir."

Rage fills me as I dash across the grass.

"Ow! What in the hell?" the man calls out.

Ann backs away. "I apologize, but I did warn you that I'm capable of defending myself."

"Viper." He wipes at blood dripping from his chin, then sees me and runs down one of the paths into the darkness.

Ann turns and gapes at me. "You saw that?"

"I'm not certain what I saw," I admit. "You are unharmed?"

"Of course." She holds up a pearl with a long metal needle. "It's a hat pin. Very handy to always have one for moments when men behave ungentlemanly." Wiping the tip on a handkerchief, she then puts the pin in her bun as if nothing is amiss.

"Why did you come out here alone? It's not safe." I want to scold her, but she's not mine.

She frowns and walks toward the house.

I step beside her and admire more than I should the swell of her breasts as she takes a deep breath.

"I was warm. You were dancing, as was Louisa. I suppose I thought at my advanced age, I would be safe." She laughs. "Perhaps I should be flattered." She brushes out her skirt.

"There is nothing about you or your age that a man will dismiss, Ann. Please don't be so foolish again." How is it possible she doesn't know how utterly delectable she is?

"I'm twenty-eight years old, Oscar. As your mother noted, I've missed my chance for marriage." She said my name without any prompting and it vibrates joyfully in my ears.

We step onto the patio. "I don't think that bloke in the garden was offering marriage."

Her chuckle, though brief, is everything.

Deep in my soul, I want to be the only person to bring her the kind of joy that produces that sound. "I've lost my mind," I mutter to myself.

"I beg your pardon, my lord?" She stops halfway across the stones.

I bow. "Forgive me. You should go in. I'll be along in a few minutes. Check on Louisa. She's danced with every twit in the room, I think."

Eyes wide, she turns and rushes inside.

How is it possible that after thirty-five years on this planet without meeting a single person of the opposite sex who intrigues me for more than a night, I've stumbled upon a woman who muddles my brain? Of course, she's not for me. No one is for me. Still, I can't help the fantasy of being the catalyst for joy to fill Ann's beautiful face each day.

Chapter Five

Ann

Unfortunately, the dowager countess remembered me from my youth, but it's not the first time and likely won't be the last. What last night proved is that Louisa is much sought after and that she is not impervious to gentlemanly charm. She liked the attention and the dancing.

Two of the gentlemen from the ball called this morning. However, I don't think Louisa has any particular regard for either. She was polite, but I detected nothing in her behavior that indicated affection.

As we stroll the park, Mae joins us, making us a foursome. "Two suitors this morning?"

"Yes, Mother." Louisa's voice is monotone.

"Men of good standing?" Mae asks.

"Sir Edward Pepperton and the Earl of Stanbridge. They were both very kind to have called." Still polite indifference with no sign of interest.

Mae sighs. "Clearly, you don't care for either one, but they are both wealthy and well-respected gentlemen. You could do worse."

"Yes, Mother." Louisa waves to a group of young women.

Her mother follows her to greet them and their mothers, but looks back to give me a nod beforehand.

"I think my sister approves of the work you've done." Oscar leans in as we continue down the parade route.

"Your niece is a lovely young woman and from a good family. If she wishes to marry, it shall not be an issue." I try to slow my pace enough to walk behind as a good servant should, but Oscar won't allow it, so I give up.

"Is that what happened in your first season, Ann? Did you not wish to marry?"

My heart feels as if someone has wrapped their fist around it. "I wanted to marry but my choice wasn't approved by my father. The gentlemen my parents chose were not approved by me. After three years, I chose the life I have now."

"Why didn't you marry the man of your choice without approval if you were smitten?" He gives no hints of his feelings when he asks such personal questions. Despite his bad behavior on the one occasion, he has been a complete gentleman since.

I can't help wondering what prompted his outburst. It's none of my business. All I have to do is my job, and in a few months, we'll hire a new steward. I'll return to Everton House and never see Oscar Stafford again. "Why do you want to know about my past, my lord?" I stress the title because he used my familiar name.

His shoulders lift and fall with a deep breath. "Forgive me. I can't seem to help myself. You have been a curiosity invading my thoughts ever since we met. There are a great many things I'd like to know about you. This seems a good place to start."

It's hard to breathe. What is he saying? Why should he be

curious about me? Before he left the house, he stated clearly enough that I'm likely a woman of bad character. "There is little to tell. The object of my desire wouldn't marry without my father's approval and the dowry that went with it."

"I'm sorry," he whispers.

"It was a long time ago." Yet the memory still cuts deep. I no longer hold any affection for the gentleman, but the words spoken then set my heart to aching when remembered.

"Perhaps your father was correct in not giving that particular man his blessing. If it was the standing and money that he adored more than you." Oscar's back is very straight, and his shoulders are pulled back. He walks with his hands behind his back, as is his habit.

With a nod, I say, "I have concurred with that in the years since. Father may have refused due to the man's lack of title, but he saved me from a marriage where I would have been the only affectionate party."

"Have you seen your parents since taking employment?"

"From time to time, my mother and I have tea. Father refuses to see me, so we meet elsewhere. She doesn't approve of my working, but she says she admires my bullheadedness." I laugh. "And now you know all there is to know about me, my lord. There is no reason for your curiosity to continue."

He grumbles something under his breath, but I can't quite make it out. "You undervalue your allure."

Allure? What can that mean? I stop and face him. "What are you playing at?"

Eyes wide, he stares at me. "I beg your pardon."

"Your approach might be different, but I'm starting to wonder if you are another version of the man in the garden." So that others in the park don't notice anything amiss, I keep my hands lightly folded in front of me and my voice just above a whisper.

His jaw shifts from side to side. "Will you follow me for a moment?"

He walks to the right, crossing the grass and disappearing under the long hanging leaves of a tree.

Looking around, I check to see if anyone is watching. I should walk on and find new employment. Damn my curiosity, I follow and duck under the branches.

Stippled light passes through the thick leaves, It's cozy and quiet in the shade.

Oscar paces a few feet away. "The second day you were at my house, my behavior was regrettable."

Unsure what to say, I hold my tongue. I can admit to my curiosity.

He stops and faces me. "I find I am extremely attracted to you, Ann. I have been since the moment I met you. Since the notion of any relationship between us must be considered ridiculous, I tried to make you hate me. If you hate me, then I am safe from my own desires."

It's possible my heart stopped beating, and I'm about to die here under this tree in Hyde Park. "Why would you be attracted to me? I'm an old maid. I have nothing to offer save a full bosom. I'm sure your lordship can find plenty of that at the local brothel." My temper and a hint of jealousy rise. "I may have chosen to become an Everton Lady, but don't suppose that makes me desperate for affection or whatever it is you mean to offer."

Storming away would be wise, but my cheeks are on fire and I hardly want all of society to know how flustered I am. Covering them with my hands, I will my emotions into submission. I close my eyes.

The heat of him fills the space in front of me. "Ann?"

Opening my eyes, I have to crane my neck to meet his gaze. "What?"

A Lady's Curves

"I know I have given you no reason to trust me. I have behaved terribly and my regrets grow larger every day. However, I am not like the man in the garden. My desire for you is honest and goes beyond the physical. While I am well aware that you would never, could never, want me in any way, it is important to me that you know that sex is not the only thing on my mind."

All my efforts to push my blush away are useless in the face of his claims. "I don't believe you."

He shakes his head. "No." Deep sadness fills his eyes. "Why would you?"

Only able to stare at him, I swallow down emotions I haven't felt since that first season. I'm already aware that my gauge of these relationships is badly tuned. There is no dowry. There is no family connection. Beyond my body, I have no value to a man like Oscar Stafford. Tears push at the corners of my eyes.

"Please don't cry." He hands me his handkerchief. "I'm going to leave you. It's not because..." He shakes his head. "You'll need to collect yourself to resume the walk." He rushes out of the seclusion of the tree's embrace.

Leaning on the large trunk, I dab my eyes, staving off an embarrassing bout of tears. Once I have my emotions in check, I return to the parade path where I find Louisa and Mae strolling.

"Are you all right, Miss Wittman?" Louisa asks.

"Yes. Thank you. I'm fine. I had a bit of dust in my eye." I force a smile and step behind the ladies.

"Where is my brother?" Mae scans the park. "Ah, there, by the river." She calls for him.

His stern expression gives nothing away, but he rejoins us, walking next to me as we return to his house.

I offer him his handkerchief back.

Pressing it back into my hand, he shakes his head.

My chest tightens. I run my finger over the embroidered O and S. Other parts of me tingle and I try not to think about the things he said under the tree. Of course, that makes me think about them even more. The heat returns to my cheeks and I set my mind to thinking about the accounting waiting for me in the study.

Mae steps beside me. "I misjudged you, and I believe I owe you an apology, Miss Wittman."

"Did you?" It takes me a beat or two to focus on the sister rather than the brother.

"Yes. I'm sorry for thinking you would be unable to assist my daughter. I have never seen her excited about the prospect of balls. She asked me to take her to the modiste. It seems one of the men she danced with last night is very fond of yellow. I have no idea how she learned such a thing, but she would like a buttery gown that he might admire enough to pay her a call." Mae shakes her head indulgently. "I'm going to take her now unless you have need of her."

"Not at all. We had a quiet evening planned as there are two more events this week that we have committed to. We'll be attending the races on Thursday and Lady Tamford's ball on Saturday. Perhaps you would care to join us?" It's nice that mother and daughter are bonding over the process of a successful season.

She cocks her head. "I am otherwise committed on Thursday, but I shall be delighted to join you at the ball."

I nod. "We shall see you then, unless you'd like to join us for supper tonight when you return Louisa to your brother's home?"

"That is most kind, but Lord Creeves and I have a dinner party to attend this evening." She takes her leave, and she and Louisa walk in the opposite direction.

I am left alone with Oscar. "I can make my way, my lord. You needn't trouble yourself." I walk faster.

Keeping pace, Oscar says, "I will see you back to my house, Miss Wittman."

"It's really not necessary." I'm flustered and I don't like it. Everton Ladies can handle any situation with aplomb.

"Ann?" His voice is sharp and he touches my arm.

I stop and look at him.

"Are you afraid of me? Was my behavior so bad that an apology and confession were not enough? Am I so abhorrent to you that there is no chance of friendship?" His eyes are filled with worry.

Everton Ladies remain detached. We don't get involved with our clients. Well, that's not always true. I can name a handful of ladies who have lovely families now with the men they once served in some domestic capacity. I am not one of them. I'm far past the blush of youth and was never a diamond of the first water. "I'm not afraid of you, Oscar. It's only that my purpose is to resolve your bookkeeping issues and help your niece with her first season. Whatever else you want seems beside the point."

A hint of a smile pulls at his lips and my heart. "I'm glad you're not afraid of me, and I am truly sorry for my behavior. Nothing I said that second day was true, nor did I ever think those things. I suppose I was afraid of you."

There's a flutter low in my belly. I like the way he looks at me and everything he said today. My vanity has risen to the surface. I push it down and continue the walk to his home. Without further conversation, we arrive at his front door and Jenkin pulls it open before we knock.

"My lord, Miss Wittman, good afternoon." The butler bows.

"Hello, Jenkin. Miss Bartholomew will be arriving later.

She's gone to the modiste with her mother. Will you see that a footman is available to help her with any packages when she arrives?" I take off my gloves and hat and clutch them in my hands. "My lord, would you like to have supper here with Louisa, Lady Chervil, and me?"

All the air seems to rush out of the foyer.

Oscar's eyes are wide. He draws a long breath. "That is most kind. I would be delighted to join you ladies for dinner. I shall return to my rooms at the club so that my valet might dress me appropriately." With a bow, he leaves.

Jenkin stares at me and I swear he's amused. I go to the study and dive into strings of numbers to avoid all the thoughts spinning in my head.

Chapter Six

Oscar

I arrive at my home in time for the daily influx of callers. Almost every day since the first ball my niece attended, some young man has called to spend time with Louisa. At first, I didn't attend because I was certain Ann wouldn't want my company. Now, however, I've been invited to dine in my own home on three occasions. The conversation has been clever and lively.

Granted, Lady Chervil fills much of the silence with amusing stories about her life.

Honestly, I'm grateful for her ladyship's presence. She keeps me from doing something stupid like kissing Ann until she understands my words under the tree in the park were sincere. It's possible I didn't make my intentions clear that day. I've tried to replay the conversation in my mind, but I was driven by emotion, and much of what was said is lost to me.

Jenkin opens the door as I reach the top step. "My lord."

"Is everything under control here, Jenkin?" It's good to have the old butler and his wife back in the house. I can't think why I let Bellston talk me into pensioning the couple. Likely out of laziness, not wishing to be bothered with the world beyond my experiments.

"The ladies have a caller in the parlor. It would seem this particular gentleman brings with him more excitement than the previous visitors." Jenkin's left eyebrow rises and that is the only indication of emotion.

"Indeed? I suppose it's good that I've come then." I hand him my hat and gloves. Everything is polished and tidy in the foyer and the rest of the house. It's a far cry from when Ann arrived a month ago.

"Will you be staying to supper, my lord?" Jenkin stands, holding my outerwear as if it's a shield and he awaits battle orders.

"If I am invited. Miss Ann has charge of this house for... now." I wanted to say for the foreseeable future, but that seemed a bit too telling.

"Very good, my lord." He bows.

I make my way to the parlor where Lady Chervil and Ann sit on the settee at one end of the room. The two seem deep in conversation.

At the other end, Louisa is speaking in low tones with a man with black hair and brown eyes. I recall her dancing with this gentleman at her first ball. I thought him dull in manner, but he appears quite animated about their conversation.

I clear my throat.

Ann stands and curtsies. Her cheeks turn a delightful shade of pink, and I wonder if it is from a desire to see me or because she and Lady Chervil were talking about me. Either way, it's lovely. "My lord."

I bow. "Hello, Miss Wittman. Lady Chervil."

Honoria doesn't stand, but she smiles. "How nice to see you, my lord. Will you take some tea?"

I nod. "I see we have a guest this morning."

Closing the gap between us, Ann says, "Phillip Dutton, the Viscount of Mansfield." She turns to the young couple. "Louisa, your uncle has arrived."

Both Mansfield and Louisa jerk their heads up and stand.

I walk over. "Mansfield, good of you to call." I shake his hand and give Ann a reassuring smile.

Phillip's grip is firm and his gaze meets mine more assuredly that most men his age. My size often intimidates people. "A pleasure to be received here, Lord Kendall. Miss Bartholomew and I were just discussing a piece of music we both share an interest in."

"I see. Do you play as well as my niece?" Her mother might be annoyed by Louisa's attention to music rather than society, but I can fully understand her desire to maintain the things she loves. Her focus on music is not dissimilar to my obsession with science.

"I play very well, but have not had the pleasure of hearing the lady play as of yet." He draws a deep breath and looks at Louisa. "I would be honored if you would play."

Eyes so wide I think she may refuse, Louisa gulps down whatever she might have said and inclines her head.

As Louisa sits at the pianoforte, Ann and Honoria join us and we all sit.

Music fills the parlor as Louisa's gentle touch draws so much beauty from the instrument. It's as if she were part of it and it was part of her. If memory serves, the piece is Vivaldi, and she's playing *Four Seasons,* though I'm not familiar enough to know the particulars. It's the most beautiful thing I've ever heard.

Lady Chervil leans over and whispers, "The viscount danced with Louisa twice at Lady Tamford's Ball."

It probably means the young man has intentions toward an offer, but I don't know him well enough. My brother-in-law will have to make that decision. Though I worry Creeves only cares about an advantageous match. I find myself more concerned with Louisa's happiness. Strange that my thinking about such matters has altered so much in the few weeks that Ann has come into my life.

Louisa stops after one of the sections and lowers her eyes.

We all applaud.

Phillip claps the loudest and then turns to me. "No, my lord, I do not play as well."

The two stare at each other and speak so quietly that I can't make out the conversation.

At a tap on the arm from Honoria, I follow the ladies to the other side of the room.

Soon, two pairs of hands are playing softly and the couple is engrossed in the music.

"He will offer. Do we know anything about him?" Honoria asks.

I'm about to say that we don't when Ann cuts me off. "He has a very nice fortune with a house in town and a reportedly lucrative estate in Surry. His family is in good standing. His father died three years ago and he is the sole heir. I could find no impropriety anywhere with relation to the viscount."

"You are thorough." Admittedly, I'm shocked by the amount of information Ann has about a man I'd never heard of. Of course, hiding away in Scotland leaves me out of touch with the ton and its people.

"It's my job, my lord." She looks across at Louisa as the music stops and Phillip stands. Is it longing I see in her gaze or is it merely what I wish to see?

"Did my sister attend the ball last night?" I need to snap myself out of this insane desire. Ann Wittman has no interest in a reclusive man who is rejected by society.

Honoria says, "She did attend and was very pleased with everything. Even your brother-in-law attended. I hadn't realized he was so reserved. I remember your sister as a very lively young woman when she first came out."

"I remember that as well." I think about how often Mae used to laugh. I suppose I laughed more in those days too.

Louisa and Phillip approach and stand silently for a moment.

Phillip says, "I must take my leave."

Ann and I stand.

Ann says, "It was good of you to come, my lord."

He bows deeply, gives one last look at Louisa, and strides from the room.

No one speaks until the front door closes and Jenkin takes up his post in the parlor doorway.

Flopping into a chair, Louisa lets out a long breath. "He's very nice and his knowledge of music is vast."

"That's good, isn't it?" I venture.

She nods. "Mother said she thought father would approve him. Father knew the last viscount and they were friends."

I look across to Ann for guidance.

She shrugs and sits back on the settee with Honoria.

Sitting in the chair next to Louisa, it hits me how little choice young ladies have in life. Ann made her own decision not to marry where she didn't love and has been ostracized by society for it. Louisa likes Phillip, but her father could easily deny him should he offer.

I've never given the subject much thought before. I'd hate it if Louisa were unhappy. "What do you want?"

"Time to decide if one man or the next will make me happy

for the rest of my life." She wipes away a tear. "I know I'm expected to marry, and I want to make my mother and father proud. I don't want to be shut into a marriage where I'm unloved and forgotten until a son is born."

It's the most I've ever heard her say. "Have you told your parents this?"

"No. Of course, not. They just want me out of their house and managing my own. If mother had had sons, it would be easier, but with three daughters, they have to hope for a male heir from one of us before Father dies, or the estates will go to a cousin none of us knows." It sounds as if all or part of that was repeated by someone else.

"What if I tell your father your wish to finish out the season before you make any decisions? Would it help?" My brother-in-law has always been cordial to me and I think he's a bit afraid of me. That could work to my advantage.

Louisa sits up straight. "Why would you do that, Uncle? Father might get angry."

"I'm not afraid of your father, but I am concerned with your future happiness."

Before I have time to draw breath, Louisa is out of her chair and leaps into my arms. "You are not at all the way Mother describes you. I think perhaps she doesn't know you at all." She stands up and pulls her shoulders back. Chin high, she says, "I will speak to my father. It's a small thing to ask for and perhaps he will see it as a way to garner more attention from worthy gentlemen."

Cunning. I had no idea. "If you need my assistance, you need only ask." As she turns to leave the parlor, I take her hand. "Louisa, I mean that in all things for the rest of my life. Should you need me, you may always call on me as your uncle to help you."

Tears fill her eyes, but she doesn't shed them. Instead, she smiles. "I think that's the nicest thing anyone has ever said to me. Thank you, Uncle Oscar." She squeezes my hand and grins before leaving the room.

Both Ann and Honoria are dabbing at the corners of their eyes.

"Well done, my lord." Honoria takes a deep breath. "I think I shall lie down before dinner. Do you need anything of me, Ann?"

"No. Go and rest." Ann smiles warmly at the dowager and watches her leave.

We sit silently for long moments. Ann will not meet my gaze, and I can't decide if she's embarrassed about something or detests me. Unable to bear the quiet, I ask, "Did I say something wrong with regard to my niece?"

Meeting my gaze, the soft pink of her cheeks heightens. "No, Oscar. You said everything right. I wish I'd had an advocate like you when I was her age."

"I don't. If you had, you might be married now rather than my Everton Lady." I blurt it out before I can think better of it.

She bites her lower lip and her breath quickens. "It's quite warm in here. Would you like to walk in your garden?"

I stand and offer my arm. Once outside, we walk along the outer path of the small garden. "My grounds in Devonshire are expansive. You will like the gardens if you enjoy walking."

"I do. We should consider going there when the weather is warmer, as that's when most of the ton will leave London. Lady Chervil will accompany us, of course." She drops her hand from the crook of my elbow.

Wanting her touch back, I take her hand in mine. We didn't stop for gloves, and her skin is soft and warm, sending a tingle through my entire body.

She gasps but doesn't pull away. "This is very intimate, my lord."

"Oscar." I kiss her fingers.

"I fear what I was going to say will be taken the wrong way now." There's an uncharacteristic shake to her voice.

"Perhaps you could trust that I will not misconstrue your words." I wrap her hand around my arm and we continue around the path.

"I thought to indicate that you would be welcome to move back into your home. I can see from the last few weeks that I was hasty in allowing you to leave. You have been very kind to not demand to return. This is your house and you would have been fully within your rights to return at any time. But you didn't."

"No. I did not wish to further harm our friendship." My pulse is hard and fast. It takes all my will to keep from kissing her.

She stops and faces me. She pulls her bottom lip through her teeth, leaving it plump and rosy. "I believe our friendship is secure."

Unable to resist any longer, I lean down and press my lips to hers. When she doesn't immediately slap my face, I cradle her cheek in my palm and slide my tongue along the seam of her lips.

Gripping my shoulders, Ann gasps and gives me access to her magnificent mouth. A low moan rumbles inside her.

I deepen the kiss, my body on fire for more of her, all of her. The thought sobers me enough that I pull back with one last chaste kiss. "I probably shouldn't have done that, but I shall never be sorry for it."

Chapter Seven

Ann

"He kissed me," I tell Honoria in her room two days after the event. It felt as if the moment was growing too large inside of me. I had to tell someone.

"He being...?" Honoria's blue eyes are already quite large and they grow wider with her gaping mouth as she stares at me from the small desk in the guest room.

It's hard to speak. My body had been on high alert ever since the kiss. Then Oscar moved back into his house the next day. I find myself searching for him and avoiding him at the same time. I should be above all of this. I'm twenty-eight years old. No man wants a woman my age for more than an affair. However, the kiss was sweet and tender. It felt as if there was promise there. *Don't be an idiot.* I focus on Honoria. "Oscar. I mean the Earl of Kendall."

She sucks her lips in as if she might be holding back a grin or laugh. "Was it a brotherly peck on the cheek or something more meaningful?"

"The latter, though I have little to compare the sensation. I'm fairly certain his tongue in my mouth indicates more than brotherly affection." I want to take it all back and run from her room. Then I want to hide in my room until I can make my escape back to Everton House. Actually, those are just the lies I tell myself. I want more of Oscar's kisses and to know what he was thinking.

"Indeed. Delicious. I'm not surprised. He looks at you with a great deal of fondness. Perhaps he loves you." Honoria uses a white puff to put powder on her nose.

"No. Of course, he doesn't love me. He likely thinks I'm lonely and he is too. A bit of affection is all it was."

Honoria cocks her head. "And are you—lonely?" One of the things I love most about her is there is no judgment with regard to the morality of kissing a man for the sake of mutual loneliness. It makes me wonder about what kind of past she might have had.

"Sometimes." I live in a house full of people and have some good friends there and around the city. Still, I find there are times late at night when my heart yearns for something more. "I'm being silly. I have all I need."

Putting down her powder puff, Honoria turns to face me. "There is nothing silly about wanting companionship or even love. You are still a young woman, Ann. Your father is no longer in control of you and hasn't been for some years."

"My father has nothing to do with this. I'm eight and twenty. Men do not marry women long on the shelf and I do not have dalliances." I draw a breath and it's shakier than I'd like. "I shouldn't have spoken of the matter. His lordship likely regrets the impulse as much as I do."

"Hmm." She turns back to the glass and sighs. "I am always

A Lady's Curves

at your disposal should you need to talk. You know that whatever you tell me, I shall take to the grave."

I get up and hug her from behind. In the glass, I look into her eyes. "You are a dear friend."

She pats my hand. "You had better get ready. We have a ball to attend."

Another ball. I sigh. I'm tired of attending celebrations where I hide in the corner like a thief. I'd much rather stay in and read a book. No. That's not true. I like balls, but without taking to the floor, it is rather a bore. However, this one is unavoidable as it is being held by Louisa's parents. "I'll go and dress. Miss Louisa has requested we arrive early so she can speak to her father."

"Oh, well, I'd better get a move on then. Will you pull the bell for my maid?" She touches her hair and frowns.

I pull the bell cord and go to my room.

Margery, Honoria's maid, is standing by the wardrobe in my room. "Margery, what are you doing here? Lady Chervil just rang for you."

She smiles and looks down at the lavender gown lying across her arms. "His lordship sent this for you. He asked if I can make any alterations that are necessary before I dress Lady Chervil tonight."

The fabric is delicate and beautiful. I'm drawn forward and touch the dyed lace along the sleeves. It also runs down the skirt. "This is very fine, but I should wear one of my dresses."

Nudging me in front of a full-length glass mirror, she puts the dress in front of me. "You will be beautiful in this, Miss Ann. Why not wear the gift? From the worried expression on his lordship's face when he gave it to me to press, I don't believe it comes with any expectations." Margery is very bold, but one would have to be to be Honoria's lady's maid.

I almost look pretty in a dress like this. "Perhaps."

She grins. "Good. Let's get you dressed. Then I'll go and do her ladyship's hair and come back to do yours."

I've lost my mind, but I agree.

We step inside the Creeves' townhouse and Mae rushes through the foyer. "I'm so glad you're here." She hugs her brother and then Louisa. She greets Honoria formally, then stops when she reaches me. "You look different, Miss Wittman."

Holding my chin up, I force a smile. "A new gown and wrap, my lady." I pull the dark purple wrap around tighter.

Scanning me from head to toe, she smiles, and then winks. "Lovely."

Louisa says, "Mother I must speak to Father before the other guests arrive."

"He is in the library. Would you like me to go with you?" Concern creases Mae's forehead.

"Yes. That would be best. I'd hate to have to do this twice." Louisa pulls her shoulders back and looks at me with a hint of her inner panic showing in her eyes.

I give her a reassuring smile and nod. "The worst he can say is no and you're no worse off than before."

Taking a deep breath, she strides down the hall behind the grand staircase with her mother following.

The butler offers to take our outerwear.

I hesitate to relinquish my wrap, but there is little choice so I give it over.

Honoria saunters toward the ballroom behind a footman.

Oscar stares at me, then a wide smile breaks across his face.

He smiles so rarely, I hardly knew how handsome he really was until this moment.

My heart pounds and my hands sweat. The riotous butterflies have broken loose in my belly. "Thank you for the gown."

"Seeing you in it is more than thanks enough. You're beautiful, Ann." He offers his arm.

Throat clogged with emotion, I slip my hand through the crook of his elbow and allow him to show me into the ballroom. We are the first to arrive, so it's not inappropriate for him to be my escort. Who would know?

"Don't you two look cozy." The Dowager Countess of Kendall strides over, carrying a cane that barely touches the ground.

I pull my arm away and curtsy. "Good to see you again, Lady Kendall."

"Mother, why are you here so early?" The brooding tone is back in Oscar's voice as he pulls his hands behind his back.

A knowing smile followed by a stern look crosses over her face. "Your sister wanted my help and so I am here. Where is your charge?"

Since her overbearing stare is on me, I say, "She has gone to speak to her father."

"Lord, she's not joining the Everton Domestic Society, is she?" The derision in her voice is lost on no one.

"Calliope, is that you?" Honoria drifts across the room to join us.

"Honoria?"

They both curtsy and then kiss cheeks.

"I had hoped to see you tonight." Honoria's smile is contagious and even Lady Kendall is susceptible.

"It's good to see you. It's been many years. I understand you are employed." There is no love in the last word.

Honoria's smile widens. "I found that life had grown dull.

Husbands dead, children grown and living their lives. I needed something to do with my time. Withering away gracefully isn't my style."

There's a longing in Oscar's mother's eyes. "I know what you mean, but taking employment. It's unseemly."

"Perhaps, but such fun." She slips her arm around Calliope and moves her across the ballroom to the chairs along the wall. "Tell me what you've been doing with your time, I'll regale you with tales of Everton House."

Watching them, I find my love for Honoria grows even deeper. She's always coming to the rescue.

"Miss Wittman?"

I'd forgotten how close Oscar was. His voice is buttery and only inches from my ear. I spin around. "My lord?"

"May I have the first dance?"

"With me?" I blink and shake my head as if that might make sense out of this evening.

He chuckles and takes my hand. Bowing, he kisses my knuckles. "With you, if you will."

"I'm here to assist Louisa, not to dance." The denial is as weak as the reasoning.

"She can spare you here in her family home. Besides, my niece has found her voice. She's going to be fine." He looks at me as if the credit falls to me, but Louisa did it on her own.

"I only offered some encouragement." A bit lightheaded, I say, "I would enjoy the dance, my lord."

He whispers, "Oscar." With a brief smile for me, he crosses to greet his brother-in-law.

The Earl of Creeves is tall and thin with stern eyes and a sharp jaw. Despite the harsh look, he seems genuinely happy to see Oscar. They shake hands and exchange a few words.

Oscar grins and nods before leaving the ballroom.

A few guests begin to enter, their voices excited for the anticipated ball.

Remembering my place, I step back until I'm hidden by a large statue decorated with white and blue flowers.

"Miss Wittman, I presume." The Earl of Creeves rounds the statue and stares down his patrician nose at me.

I curtsy. "Lord Creeves. I am Ann Wittman. A pleasure to meet you."

"I admit to curiosity about you and your profession after hearing much about you from my wife and now my daughter." He bows. "The pleasure is mine."

Keeping my shoulders back and my chin up, I meet his gaze despite my pounding heart. "I hope whatever you have heard did not displease you, my lord."

"On the contrary. They both esteem you greatly. My daughter has asked me to give her until the end of the season to choose a husband. She has informed me that she favors Lord Mansfield, but would like time to decide her future. She made a compelling argument." He steps next to me and watches the partygoers file in.

"She is a very bright young lady." I keep my other thoughts to myself as I wish to know how Louisa's proposal was received before I make my opinion known.

With his arms crossed over his chest, he looks grave, but a hint of a smile shines in his eyes. "She is. I was only blessed with daughters, Miss Wittman. I want them to have security and perhaps have sons, that one of them might inherit should my cousin precede me in death. More than security, I wish them to be happy." He waves at the air as if words are hanging there. "I know society brands me heartless, but I do care that Louisa and her sisters live happy lives." After a long pause, he clears his throat. "I have granted Louisa the time she requested and when offers come, as it seems they will, I shall tell the gentlemen they must wait until the last week of this season for my answer."

"That is very good of you, my lord." Excitement thrums in my chest. I could not be prouder of Louisa.

"You have brought her out of her shell, as they say, Miss Wittman. I am grateful. Should you need a letter of recommendation at any point or my assistance in any way, you need only ask." He faces me and bows.

"That is most kind. Thank you."

"I have asked Louisa to come home when you and Lord Kendall go to the country. As it shall be our last few months with her, I would like to have her here. She didn't object." He lets a hint of a smile slip before returning to his mild expression.

The music begins and Mae waves her husband to the floor where they will lead the first dance.

"I believe I have this dance, Ann." Oscar's voice is low and intimately close to my ear.

Chapter Eight

Oscar

Somehow, I must master my feelings for Ann. She would no sooner want me than my old uncle Jeremiah. Kissing her was foolish. Buying the gown, well, that was pure selfishness. I can't regret it.

I lie on the settee in my study, grateful to be back in my home. My valet went to bed. I decided I would not lay another night staring at the heavy curtains, praying for sleep while wishing for Ann. Not that lying here is much better. The memory of holding her in my arms while we danced is so fresh that it's unlikely I'll sleep tonight.

The creaking of the door opening rouses me.

Ann pads in and goes to the bookshelf behind the library ladder. She runs her fingers along the spines while holding a candle high enough to read the titles. In a white gown and wrap, with her dark hair lying over her shoulders, she looks more angel than woman.

"Can you not sleep?" I speak softly.

She jumps, barely holding on to the candlestick. "My lord, what are you doing in here so late?"

My shirt is pulled from my trousers, and I've removed my boots. I'm hardly presentable, but I round the settee anyway. She's my true north, and I can't stay away. "Sleep eluded me as well."

Her hand still lies across the rise of her breasts. "I thought a book might help."

My body continues toward her despite my resolve to keep my distance. "Would you like to know what keeps me awake?"

The way her nose scrunches as she thinks is adorable. "If you would like to tell me, my lord."

"My name is Oscar." Foolishly, I touch her soft cheek.

Leaning into my touch, she whispers, "Oscar, why can you not sleep?"

There are only inches between us. The heat of her body seeps through my clothes and I cup her jaw. "Because my thoughts always turn to you. I long to know what you think and what you're doing. I ache to touch you and learn of your past."

Her breath catches. "I am not at all interesting."

I take the candlestick from her hand and place it on the table. Threading my fingers through her hair, I relish the silky feel. "I find you very much so. I have no right to the desires rushing through me. I'm a man who hides away in Scotland to avoid society. Yet, one look at you and I've become someone I barely recognize."

"Perhaps you are ill. It might pass by morning." She leans her cheek into my touch.

"It has been many mornings now and it has not passed. In fact, my attraction to you has only grown stronger." I wait and hope for some sign from her that she wants my touch.

Breasts rising and falling fast, she bites her bottom lip. "You want me?"

"I do." My cock is painfully in agreement and if she draws much closer, she'll have no doubt as to the nature of my physical attraction.

"I'm not ignorant of what happens between a man and a woman, though I've never experienced such a thing." Her cheeks are bright red, but her gaze is as direct as ever.

"You haven't run from the room even though you could have, should I take that as some indication that you are at least curious about lovemaking with me?" It's too much to hope for and not enough to offer. "I hope you know that my intentions will always be honorable."

She cocks her head and her expression is perplexed. When the realization dawns, she backs up a step. "I wouldn't expect such a gesture, Oscar." As if missing my touch, she closes the gap and brushes her fingers along the open vee in my shirt. "I thought men rushed in when a woman left herself vulnerable as I have done here tonight."

My body is on fire. "I promise that as soon as I have your permission, I will do exactly that, but not before, Ann."

Biting that full beautiful lip again, she lets her wrap fall to the floor. She pulls the bow at the ruffled neckline of her nightgown and lets it pool at her feet. "You have my permission, though you'll have to instruct me on how to proceed."

Full and lush, her body is everything a man could want. Rounded and luscious in all the right places, she's perfection.

Any remnants of my resolve to remain a gentleman fall away. I take her hand and lead her to the settee. "You are the most beautiful woman, Ann." I strip out of my clothes and let her look at me.

Her eyes widen, but I see no fear in their depths. "I'm not at all certain what I've been told will be possible. You are quite a bit larger than I imagined."

Easing her back onto the cushion, I kneel on the floor and

kiss her. Her mouth is warm and her tongue explores mine. I kiss her neck. "I promise it is possible. You're going to have to trust me. Can you do that?"

"I do trust you." She runs tentative fingers along my shoulder and down my arm.

Those four words are everything. Nothing has ever made me feel more humbled or happier in my entire life. I kiss a path down her chest and suck one perfect nipple into my mouth.

She grips my hair and squeaks, stifling whatever noise tries to get out.

I long to hear her scream my name, but she's right. The house may be asleep, but if we are indiscreet, servants will come to investigate.

Her full breast overflows my hand as I massage and suck, then lick and give the other the same adoration. "I could drown in your body, Ann."

Arching her back, she pants and tightens her fists.

The pain of pulled hair only adds to my desire, but I want her pleasure first. Sliding my hand between her legs, I find her wet folds and tease her bud.

Her body jerks, and she pants. "Oscar. Oh, that's…"

Needing more, I move to pull her legs over my shoulders and slip my tongue between her folds. She tastes like nectar from the gods, and I lick and suck until she's writhing beneath me.

Her heels dig into my back and her sheath pulses around the tip of my tongue as her pleasure crashes.

"What. Oh." She shudders.

I rise from the floor and hold her as the orgasm rolls through her. "You are the most beautiful creature ever made."

Running her hands up and down my back, she says, "That was wonderful, Oscar. Will you show me the rest?"

My cock jerks between us. Meeting her gaze, I notch

myself at her center. "It may hurt this one time, Ann, but never again."

She nods and lifts her hips to bring me in.

Pressing forward, I fill her.

She cries out and digs her nails into my shoulders. "I'm alright." Her voice sounds near tears.

Taking her lips with mine, I kiss her slowly but keep my body still. It's the sweetest torture, but I wait for her pain to pass. I pull her bottom lip between mine, and then the top one.

She lifts her hips, taking more of me and moans low against my mouth.

"You are perfect." I ease back and fill her again and again.

It takes all my will to keep silent as my pleasure builds. When her body pulses around my cock, I can't hold back anymore. I pound harder and faster, bringing my pleasure to a crescendo. At the last moment, I reluctantly pull free and spill my seed between us.

Her intake of breath is shaky. "That was more than I expected. So much more."

I maneuver us so that I can sit and pull her into my lap. Brushing her hair away from her eyes, I kiss her cheek. "I hope that's a good thing."

Nodding she blushes. "It was wonderful, Oscar." '

"I wish I could spend the night holding you in my arms." I hug her, reveling in the way her body fits against mine.

She sighs. "I should go to my bed. If we are discovered, it would be disastrous."

Part of me wishes we would be found and the things she worries about would no longer be in our hands. I know Everton ladies are not meant to have relations with their clients. The organization would be sullied. Even though her reasoning is clear to me, I don't like the idea of being considered a mistake.

"Stay a moment longer, please." I hold her tighter and snuggle against her luscious breasts.

Hugging my neck, she says, "Just another moment." There's a dreamy quality to her voice.

This woman will be my ruination. Still, I would risk everything to stay as we are right now. "I would like to show you my home in Scotland. I think you would like it there."

"I think we must go to Devonshire." She lets out a long breath and pushes off of my lap. She crosses to her nightgown and pulls it over her head.

As she ties the bow at her throat, I long to sweep her into my arms and carry her to my bed. I have to close my eyes to keep the urge at bay. "Of course. Kensfield Manor is a fine holding. It is only that the nature of Scotland is magnificent."

Putting on her wrap, she again is angelic, though I much prefer her wanton and pressed against me. Her voice has lost its softness. She is back to being an Everton Lady. "I will have the books for this house and the one in Scotland sorted within the week. There was little damage to the finances in the north. You are fortunate to be very wealthy. You will survive this situation."

I pull on my trousers and shirt. "I will walk you to your room."

"No. Someone might see us. You should stay here until I'm gone for a few minutes. I can make my own way." Looking at the door and the desk, she avoids my gaze. "I will see you tomorrow, my lord."

Before she can make her escape, I cut her off and touch her chin so that she will look at me. "I am Oscar, Ann. We have shared something quite beautiful, don't become formal to protect yourself. You need no protection from me."

A warm smile lightens her face. She cups my cheek. "Good night, Oscar."

I kiss her forehead and breathe in her scent before stepping aside and watching her leave the study.

Returning to my bed, I can think of nothing but Ann. However, now all my thoughts are warm and wanting. Somehow, I will find a way to make this right. Though for the life of me, I can't see how. She deserves a man who will give her back the life she gave up.

She already turned down a life full of all the things she was raised to believe were important. She did so in the name of love. Then that love was proved false. If I could find that blaggard, I would call him out.

I suppose the question that must be answered is how do I prove that my feelings are sincere?

Determined to do everything in the right way, I consider a plan. It would be wise to refrain from any more intimacies. Though I'm only human and she is a goddess. It's foolish to make promises which I know I cannot keep, and turning down Ann's luscious body is impossible.

Perhaps it would be smart to let things cool off. I can busy myself outside the house. At least until it's time to go to the country estate.

Sure that my short-term plan is right, I close my eyes and consider a longer campaign.

Chapter Nine

Ann

Morning came far too soon. It took a long time to fall asleep after making love with Oscar. I can hardly believe what I allowed to happen and yet find it impossible to regret it.

Staring down at my work, the numbers all blur as my mind drifts back to how wonderful it felt to be naked in his arms.

"Ridiculous." I must be sensible. It was never likely that I would experience sexual intercourse, and I must treat the moment as a past adventure. There's no point in looking forward to more.

According to Mrs. Jenkin, Oscar left the house just after dawn. He clearly doesn't wish to have the awkward moment of seeing me this morning.

It's for the best. Still, my chest hurts.

Refocusing on my work, I shake off the useless feelings and add the ledger column.

For a few hours, I managed quite nicely and even the sound

of the front door knocker and talking in the foyer is only faintly registered.

The study door swings open. Mae Bartholomew stands on the threshold beaming. "You did it!"

Placing my quill in the holder, I stand. "What did I do, my lady?"

The normally standoffish countess rushes forward and throws her arms around me. "Thank you. I can't thank you enough."

Dumbfounded, I pat her back for lack of another option. "I'm glad you're pleased, but I have no idea what has put you in such a euphoric state."

Mae pulls back and straightens the little wine-colored jacket that matches her day dress. "Forgive me. I'm just so relieved. Lord Creeves received two requests for Louisa's hand last night. Two."

"That's flattering for her. Shall I call her and order some tea?" I escort Mae across the foyer to the parlor and pull the cord near the door.

Nodding, Mae sits on the settee grinning. "I hope she'll be pleased."

I sit opposite, on one of the overstuffed chairs.

Mrs. Jenkin comes a moment later.

"Will you ask Miss Louisa to join us and have the cook make some tea please, Mrs. Jenkin?" I have butterflies in my stomach and I can't say why. It's not as if I'm the one on the marriage mart.

Once Louisa arrives, she kisses her mother's cheek. "I didn't think I'd see you today, Mama."

"I have news." Mae is the most animated I've ever seen her. She struggles to contain a grin and folds and unfolds her hands. "Both the Viscount of Mansfield and Sir Edward Pepperton went to your father for permission to marry you during the ball last night."

Face frozen, Louisa looks between tears and laughter. "Oh. I didn't think it would be so soon."

Mae's smile falters. "I thought you liked the viscount."

"I do. What did Father say?" She grips the edge of the settee with white knuckles.

"He told them both that they were not the only suitors who had shown interest, and he would not give any answer until closer to the end of the season. He said that he had promised you a full season and if they wished to call on you that would be acceptable." Mae looks at her daughter with love and pride.

It breaks my heart a little, as I wish my mother had looked at me that way. I suppose she would have if I had done as I was told.

The arrival of the tea forces us all into silence until Dotty, the downstairs maid, leaves. She looks back at us with concern but closes the door behind her.

In a very short time, Louisa has earned the affection of the entire staff in her uncle's home.

A small grin and blush push away the worry on Louisa's sweet face. "I do like the Viscount, and we have much in common."

"And Sir Edward?" Mae asks.

Louisa wrinkles her nose. "He's a nice gentleman, but speaks mostly of hunting and his country estate and how it relates to hunting. There is little for me to respond on the subject. He doesn't care for art and is only mildly interested in music. The Viscount plays very well and is well-versed in art and literature. He spoke about his estates, but only concerning their locations and what he likes about each region. It would be nice to marry someone who I can converse with on a variety of subjects."

Mae takes a deep breath and her smile cannot be contained. "It would indeed, my dear."

During tea, it was decided that Louisa would return to her parents' home immediately rather than wait until her uncle left for Devonshire.

Her maid packed her case and by midafternoon, she hugged me goodbye and left.

Honoria dabs the corner of her eye as we stand on the front steps and watch Louisa's carriage roll to the other side of Mayfair. "I will miss that one. Sweet girl. She'll do very well."

"It makes sense for her suitors to call on her at her family's home." I see the logic, but the house feels empty with her gone and no sign of Oscar all day.

Sighing, Honoria sashays back inside. "Where is his lordship?"

I follow. "I don't know."

"Did you quarrel?" She saunters into the parlor, looks at the clock, shrugs at the four-thirty hour, and pours a sherry from the cart.

"Of course not. What would we have to quarrel over?" I decline when she lifts the decanter in askance. Sitting at the pianoforte, I play a few cords before closing the lid over the keys.

"I don't know." Honoria sits with her sherry and crosses her ankles, swinging her legs as they don't reach the floor when she sits all the way back on the cushion. It's very childlike and rather endearing. "I thought you both looked rather friendly when I saw you dancing last night. Two dances, if I'm not mistaken. He bought you a gown and singled you out. With what you told me about the kiss, I thought perhaps a romance was blossoming."

My cheeks are on fire, but I look her in the eye. "That's ridiculous. What would an earl want with a spinster? Besides, I have made my choices."

She stares at me for a long moment. "I'm glad to hear there is no quarrel." She sips her sherry with a gentle smile pulling at her lips. "How much more work do you have on the accounts of this house?"

"Not much. A few days at most. The damage is not as bad as we first thought. While the old steward did take some money, he did not run up debt with his lordship's credit. That is a small blessing. The entire thing makes little sense." I look at the cart with the glasses and sherry and wonder if a drink would make me feel less worried about the foolish choices I've made in the last twenty-four hours.

"What do you mean?" Finishing the drink, she leans forward and places the crystal glass on the table. In her pink dress with many layers of material, she looks like a flower sitting on the green velvet settee.

"Why ruin your career as Bellston did and take only five thousand pounds? He could have taken much more and I'm sure he had to pay off the butler and housekeeper whom he hired." I've been puzzling over the matter for weeks and it makes no sense. He could live for a while on that money, but not indefinitely, and he'll find it nearly impossible to find a new position without the earl's referral.

"Didn't you tell me that a maid ran away with him?" Honoria raises an eyebrow.

"You think this is about love?" I can't fathom throwing everything away over a woman.

"Or lust. Either way, don't look so shocked. You, of all people, should understand. Didn't you give up everything you knew to be with the man you loved in that first season?" There is only caring in her voice and soft expression. Others have taunted, but Honoria only means to make a point.

"Only to find that without my dowry, his love was fleeting." Even all these years later, it stings.

She sighs. "Because he never truly loved you and you were misled. I would advise not to let one man's bad character ruin all of your life."

A bitter laugh escapes before I can stifle it. "At eight and twenty, I'm afraid your advice is too late, my lady. However, I appreciate that you care and are my dearest friend."

Popping up, she flounces back to the cart with her glass. "Are you certain you wouldn't like to join me?"

What harm can it do to have a sherry a bit earlier than is custom? "Thank you. I will have a small one."

Grinning, she pours.

─── ∘ ───

For the second day in a row, morning came far too early. My head is splitting and as punishment, I force myself to go out into the garden and brave the sunshine.

Honoria kept pouring, and I kept drinking. I barely remember dinner or much else of the evening.

Finding a shady spot under a tree, I slump onto the bench and hold my head in my hand.

"Are you ill, Ann?" Oscar's voice is like a balm. Deep and soft, I could listen to him all day.

Foolish woman, that's what I am. I force my gaze to his. "I took too much sherry and perhaps Lady Chervil poured some other spirits last night. My head and my stomach wish we were back in bed."

His laughter is not as pleasant as his voice. "That must have been a sight. I'm sorry I missed it."

"I am not sorry for that." I put my head back down, wishing for nightfall at ten in the morning.

His hand reaches into my gaze. "Come on."

I stare at the large yet gentle hand. "Where are we going?"

"I will have cook fix you a remedy." He wiggles his fingers.

Taking his hand, I let him help me to my feet. Part of me thinks I should suffer for my stupidity, but the rest of me can't resist the lure of his touch. "You're not going to make me drink something terrible, are you?"

He leads me through the garden and into the kitchen through the servants' door. "It's not bad actually, and it works every time."

I follow along and sit at the table where the cook writes her menus while Oscar whispers in her ear.

Mrs. Jones, the cook, is a slight woman with red hair and freckles. She's not married, but as the cook is given the honor of the *Mrs.* title. She gives me a pitiful look. "I'll get you fixed up, Miss."

"Thank you, Mrs. Jones. I'm sorry to take you away from your work." I should have some dignity, but my elbow rests on her little desk and my head feels so weighted down, that I rest it in my palm. I spy a bucket in the corner and think I could make it there should I become ill. The idea of that happening in front of Oscar keeps my lips pressed together.

Oscar leans on the wall beside me. His finger grazes my shoulder as if he's reassuring me that he's there, but also so discreet that no one on the servants' level would think anything was untoward.

A few minutes pass, and I'm soothed by the feel of him near me and the stillness of resting in the kitchen.

"Here you are, Miss Wittman." She puts a mug on the desk.

The scent is floral and it's a buttery yellow color. "What is it?"

"Tea with lavender, ginger, a few spices, and an egg." She crosses her arms and stares at me. "Don't look so sour. It tastes nice and will cure what ails you. Though, you should know better at your age not to drink so much."

I laugh and grip the handle of the mug. "You're right, Mrs. Jones. I had no business trying to keep up with her ladyship and now I've paid the price."

Grinning, she points at the drink. "That will lessen the cost. I promise."

The tea is foamy and I take a sip. "It's quite nice."

Mrs. Jones nods and returns to the long work table where she fusses with some dough.

The concoction is silky and the ginger is the standout flavor. I drink it all and like a strange miracle, my stomach settles. "That's amazing."

Once I've thanked the cook, I follow Oscar upstairs.

He stops in the hallway and takes my hand. "Feeling better?"

"Much better. Thank you." I feel well enough to be embarrassed. "I should go and check on Lady Chervil."

Chuckling, he nods. "I think her ladyship has much experience in such things and the morning after."

"Unlike me, who is still ignorant at my advanced age." I take my hand back and clasp both together to dispel the temptation to touch him. "I will be able to finalize the bookkeeping here in a few days. I'll write up a full report of your losses and the current state of this property as well as your Scotland estate."

The joy leaves his eyes and his shoulders slump. "That will be very helpful. Do you think you'll be ready to go to Devonshire in a week's time?"

"I'll check with Lady Chervil, but that should be fine." It should be a good thing that we are talking business, but I want to cry.

Straightening, his jaw ticks. "I will write to the butler at Kensfield Manor and tell him we'll need the house opened up and two guest rooms readied." He bows and rushes down the hall toward the stairs.

I listen to his heavy boots climbing to the upper level. How have I made such a mess of this assignment? I've been a fool, but no longer. I will behave like an Everton Lady. In a few weeks or a month, I'll have the work done and I'll be out of Oscar's life forever.

That should make me feel relieved, but sorrow fills my heart.

I suppose I should tell my mother that I'll be in Devonshire. It might be possible to visit with her if Father isn't home. It's a big enough area that it's unlikely I'd run into them on the street, but still, the idea of going home gnaws at my gut.

"All will be well," I tell myself and head to the study.

Chapter Ten

Ann

After two days of travel where Oscar and I said little to each other, I'm relieved to step out of the carriage in Exeter. It's market day and bustling with activity. Honoria and I walk around smelling flowers and admiring the fruits and vegetables.

Oscar said he had to meet someone and would be only an hour. His house is only ten miles from town and I'll be grateful to be out of the carriage for a good while.

"It's nice to stretch our legs," I say.

"Indeed. I've always liked Devonshire. I wonder if we might go to Plymouth. I've not been in years and I do so love the sea." Honoria smiles and turns her face up to the sun.

"It's only a day's ride, I'm sure we can manage a trip."

We stroll on and Honoria buys some sweets and a bottle of something, which she seems very pleased about. "For my health," she says, patting the sack.

"As long as it's for you and not me, I don't mind. I'm never drinking spirits with you again." I can't help laughing at her look of indignation.

She huffs. "You are a grown woman. You could have halted at any time."

"I cannot argue with that. The blame was my own and I paid the price the next morning." Remembering how sweet Oscar was and how he arranged for the cook to help me makes those butterflies active in my belly and my cheeks heat.

Honoria points across the square. "There is his lordship now."

A very determined Oscar Stafford frowns as he strides toward us. "Shall we continue our journey, ladies?"

"Is everything all right, my lord?" I ask as he escorts us back to the carriage.

His expression softens, and he lets out a long breath. "I checked with the magistrate to see if Mr. Bellston remained in this area so that I could confront him, but he has moved on. It seems he made off with some city funds."

"Oh dear." I step into the carriage. Once he's across from Honoria and me, I ask, "Did you tell him about your troubles?"

"I felt I had to." His brow is drawn in and his jaw ticks while he rings his hands.

Leaning forward, I put my hand over his. "You did the right thing." Realizing we are not alone, I pull away and avoid looking at Honoria.

Leaving town behind, the countryside is beautiful.

Maybe a change of subject would lighten the mood. "Lady Honoria has made a request that at some point we journey to Plymouth."

"Of course. Perhaps in a week or so. Have you friends there, my lady?" Oscar remains stoic, but the anger has left his eyes.

She shrugs. "I did have some friends there. I'll write and see if they're still in the area."

The first glimpse of Kensfield Manor takes my breath away. It's a sprawling house with three stories and the sun gleaming off the windows. A lake reflects the house and sky, making it even more magical. At the center of the golden stone building is a wide entry with six stairs leading to a magnificent arched double door. A dozen servants stand at the bottom of the steps awaiting our arrival. At the door, a butler with black hair, a straight back, and a stern look, stands with his hands behind his back.

Oscar leans toward me. "What do you think, Ann?"

"It's beautiful." I'm breathless.

Honoria clears her throat. "A fine property, my lord. I'm surprised you prefer the house in Scotland when you have such a home."

He's saved from answering by the carriage stopping and a footman opening the door.

Oscar steps down and waits to hand each of us out of the carriage. "Ladies, welcome to Kensfield Manor. I've not been here in years, but it is the property that pays the bills. Let's hope it's in better shape than the London house was."

The staff is bright and happy to see us. Footmen run to help the second carriage that carries Honoria's maid and Oscar's valet along with all the luggage.

At the top the stairs, Oscar shakes the butler's hand. "Hodgins, it's good to see you."

"Welcome home, my lord. The house is ready for guests." He bows to Honoria and me.

"Hodgins took over for his father as butler here about twenty years ago. Allow me to introduce Lady Honoria Chervil and Miss Ann Wittman. Miss Wittman is going to sort out the damage done by Bellston." Oscar's grimace is back.

"Very good. Mrs. Dunning will show the ladies to their rooms and there's a small meal ready whenever you've settled in. You must be tired after such a long journey." Hodgins is the perfect butler. Serious yet concerned.

I like him immediately. "Thank you, Hodgins. You've thought of everything."

A hint of a smile pulls at the butler's tight lips. "It is my honor to serve you, Miss."

Mrs. Dunning is a tall, robust woman with the keys to the house jangling at her waist. She smiles brightly. "I hope you will both like the rooms we arranged. If you need anything at all, pull the cord and someone will come to help. Will the miss be needing a lady's maid during her stay?"

It's not an unusual question. I've been asked as well as chastised for not having one. It's too much like my old life. "No thank you. My clothes are made to be donned by me alone. However, should I need help, I'll ring."

Once in my lovely room with pale-blue damask walls and matching drapes, I look out the window at the garden and the stable beyond. It's lovely here. My parents live about twenty miles in that direction.

A knock on my open door breaks me away from my thoughts.

Oscar stands just outside the doorway. "Is this to your liking, Ann? There are many other rooms if you don't care for this one."

I cross to him. "This one is very nice."

"You look as if something is wrong. In fact, I sensed through the entire journey that you were not yourself."

I could lie and say there is nothing wrong and he's mistaken. But his expression is so sincere and kind, I can't bear to lie. "My father's home is not far from here and to avoid him, I have rarely entered the county. However, I must be here and I will do all that I can to help you, my lord."

Slowly, he crosses the threshold and stands inches from me. "My name is Oscar. I am sorry that this trip has made you uncomfortable."

My discomfort is immeasurable with him so close, but not unpleasant. My body responds to our proximity in ways only Oscar elicits, as all my blood goes south and I have to squeeze my thighs together. "Oscar, Lady Chervil is just next door. Perhaps you shouldn't be in here."

His lips quirk into a half smile. "Will you come downstairs for something to eat?"

I nod. "I would like to rest for a few minutes first."

Bowing, he backs away. "Take all the time you need."

Once he is gone, I miss him. I'm such a fool.

Oscar

Having Ann at Kensfield makes the place so much more tolerable. So much so that I can't quite remember what I disliked about the estate. I spent most of my youth in these ornate rooms and halls. Yet, the first time I was allowed to go to Scotland with my father, I decided that Bielddubh was where I would settle when the title came to me.

The name of the Scottish hunting lodge means black shelter and it fits perfectly. Large and dark, it has been the perfect place to see and commune with the natural world.

Yet as I stand at the library window, looking out on the gardens and grounds beyond Kensfiled, there is much to like.

"How did he manage this?" Ann asks from my father's desk.

I suppose it's my desk now, but it's hard to think of the behemoth as mine. Dark wood that stretches eight feet wide. Ann looks confident in my father's chair, just as she did in London. Perhaps she fits no matter where she is. "Have you found something?"

Shaking her head, she studies the ledger. "I don't know. Yes. Maybe. I found an entry for the farmer's seed."

"That's not unusual. I always supply the seed for my leased farms. It gives the families a little boost." It seems a small thing. My father did the same. I know it's not conventional, but why does Ann look as if it's broken the bank?

"The issue is that I don't see the receipt for buying the seed, Oscar. I've looked through everything a dozen times. I'm missing several other receipts as well."

I stand behind her and look at the ledger. Her hair and skin are scented with roses and the warmth fills me. "What other entries are you looking at?"

She points to a column. "Here are several entries for items purchased for a Lady Day celebration."

"I know it's an old tradition that no one follows these days, but it's been part of Kensfield for generations." The amounts for food and drink do seem a bit high, but it all goes to the community.

"There are no receipts for any of those expenses." She runs her fingers down another line. "And this list of people who were given Christmas hams, I don't see the corresponding bill from the pig farmer or butcher." She turns her neck to look up at me and that brings her lips so close, it's maddening. "Will you call Hodgins?"

If I don't step away, I'm going to kiss her in broad daylight with the library doors wide open for anyone to see. I step back and pull the cord.

A minute later, Hodgins walks in. "My lord, how may I be of service?"

"Miss Wittman and I are wondering about the Christmas hams from last year. Who supplied them?" I have a knot in my gut.

For the first time in all the years I've known the butler, he looks shocked. Wide-eyed, his mouth opens and closes twice before he speaks. "The hams were canceled, my lord."

My heart sinks. "By whom?"

He blinks back at me. "By you, my lord."

It takes everything within me to keep my temper. If I think too hard about the families who went without a ham last holiday, I'll show a side of myself that I do not like. "And the Lady Day celebration?"

Hodgins dark eyes grow even wider, and he shifts his weight from foot to foot. "It too was canceled. Sir, I received a letter from you on both occasions explaining that there were some cutbacks." He looks from me to Ann, then back at me. Turning, he closes the library door and steps close to the desk. "From the expression on your faces, I'm guessing the letters were not from you. Does this have something to do with the departure of Mr. Bellston?"

The secret keeping has to stop. I can see that now. "I'm afraid, Bellston and several of the staff he hired in London made free to take what they liked. I didn't know about the hams or the celebration, Hodgins. The fault is with me, as I should have taken more care."

Ann clears her throat. "Mr. Hodgins, would you know if the annual seed allotment was delivered to the farmers in the spring?"

Shifting uncomfortably, Hodgins shakes his head. "It was quite an uproar at the time. I am sorry, my lord."

"Thank you, Hodgins. Will you have my horse brought around? It seems I have some overdue apologies to make." I don't know how I'm going to fix this, but I will.

With a nod, the butler exits and I swear I saw a hop in his step that I'd not seen before.

Ann touches my hand. "It's not really as bad for you as it might have been. I think he only took the money from those items. Perhaps you might compensate the farmers by reducing payment by what they had to put out for seed."

It's a good start. "I can't make up for a ruined Christmas dinner."

"No." She sighs. "But perhaps we could throw a nice party for the community. The weather has been very fine. We could make it a picnic with food and pony rides for the children." Her cheeks pinken and her eyes light up.

"That's a fine idea, Ann. Would you help me plan it?" Unable to resist, I run my fingers along her jaw and press my lips to hers.

She opens for me and when her tongue meets mine, I pull her into my arms and deepen the kiss.

Voices in the hallway are like a bucket of cold water, and I pull back. "Much more of that and it will be difficult to ride a horse."

Her giggle is infectious. "I will be happy to help you, Oscar."

I know she's talking about a picnic, but my heart and body consider what else she might mean.

Chapter Eleven

Ann

The sun is low on the horizon but the weather is so beautiful and I've been cooped up in the library all day. Luckily, it is a very fine library. I walk past the tall shrubs that form a wall around the estate garden. There's a dirt path and I follow it as I deserve a little exploration after a hard day's work.

I follow the sound of ducks and birds to a wooded area that surrounds a pond. It's lovely.

A splash draws my attention to the right.

Oscar's head comes up from the water.

I gasp.

His gaze meets mine.

I back up a step. Lord, he's not wearing a shirt. I'll not be able to resist him. I don't even want to. "Forgive me. I don't want to intrude on your solitude." I turn to flee.

"Don't go." The plea stops me.

Unable to resist, I look over my shoulder. "We could be

discovered here. You are not properly dressed." I scan the edge of the pond and find his clothes neatly folded on a rock, trousers included. My cheeks and neck are on fire.

He swims toward me. "No one comes here except me." His smile is wicked. "And it would seem you."

"I heard ducks." It is a ridiculous thing to say. Please let a rogue lightning bolt strike me.

"Would you like to swim with me?" He points toward his clothes. "You can leave your dress there. The water is delightful."

I walk around the pond, never taking my attention from him, and he turns to watch me the entire time. I've most certainly lost my mind, but I long to be in his arms and once this assignment is over, I'll never be asked such a thing by Oscar or any man again.

Tugging free the laces of my dress, I step out and lay it on top of his clothes. I roll down my stockings and remove them with my shoes, then pull the chemise over my head.

Naked, I stare at him and step one foot in the cool water. "I've never done such a reckless thing in my life."

Swimming closer, he stands and his shoulders breach the surface. "I'm honored to have your trust."

As I step deeper, he comes closer until he's submerged to the waist and it's a bit deeper for me. My breasts bob at the top of the water.

Oscar wraps his arm around me and lowers his head to take one of my nipples into his mouth.

I have to bite my lip to keep from crying out. "Oscar." I thread my fingers through his head. "Oh, why can't I resist you?"

He sprinkles kisses across my chest and up my neck. "I sincerely hope it's because you don't wish to, Ann. I know that

I've longed for more of you these weeks. Trying to be a gentleman has been torturous."

His tongue skims the shell of my ear and my body is on fire. I grip his back and pull myself in, wrapping my legs around him. I offer my lips, and he devours them. Kissing Oscar is like finding air when there has been none. I can't get enough of him. I need more.

His cock presses hard between our bodies. Gripping my bottom, he carries me out of the water.

"I'm too heavy."

In his green eyes, a woman could get lost. The way he looks at me is both tender and lustful. "You're perfect." Putting me on my feet on the soft grass near our clothes, he digs out his coat and spreads it on the ground. "Will you lie down?"

With my legs shaking from either lust or fear of being discovered, I'm more than happy to lie back on his coat. "How can you be certain no one will come looking for us?"

Beautifully naked, he stretches out beside me. "No one ever comes here."

"I did." I run my hand down his broad chest.

He kisses my cheek. "I'm glad you did. If you're uncomfortable, Ann, we can dress and go back to the house." He kisses my neck, trailing his tongue along my pulse and along my collarbone.

My breath is shallow and quick. Everywhere he kisses me burns for more and my womanhood aches to be touched. "I trust you, Oscar."

Stopping, he lifts his head and looks into my eyes. "You can trust me. I will never hurt you or allow anyone else to."

Women speak of the promises men make in such situations. Still, he sounds so sincere, I almost believe him. "Will you show me how to please you?"

"You cannot know how your being here naked with me

makes me feel, or you wouldn't ask that question." He runs his hand between my breasts, down my abdomen, and slides two fingers between my folds.

Pleasure fills me and I let my legs fall open. He spreads my folds and rubs my bud until I'm writhing. I bite my lip to keep from screaming. "Oh, Oscar. I'm. Oh."

"I would love to hear you let go and scream out your pleasure, love." Sliding a finger inside me, he works my flesh until I'm close to ecstasy.

"I need. Oscar." Pleasure swamps me, cascading through my entire body and culminating between my thighs.

Covering my mouth with his, he swallows my screams of pleasure. Gentling the kiss, he pulls me close, then rolls so that I'm straddling his hips.

Not sure what to do, I stare at him as the last shudder of pleasure races through me. "I don't know what you want."

Running his finger through my tussled hair, he lifts his hips so his shaft slides along my slit. "I want you to do as you please, love. You are in control."

There is something quite heady in having power over a man like Oscar. Rising to my knees, I center him at my entrance, and lower until he fills me.

He cries my name over and over like his most ardent prayer. Gripping my hips, he holds me in place, his eyes closed. A moment later, he releases me.

I rise and fall, rise and fall. Every time he fills me, my body tightens. The base of his shaft rubs against my bud. My body is on fire. I quicken the pace, chasing the pleasure I never knew existed before Oscar. Now I need it like my next breath. Throwing my head back, I ride him hard and fast, until I can't wait another second and my body squeezes his shaft, milking more delight.

"Oh, Ann. Ooohhh." Gripping my hips, he pulls me up and

off before hugging me tight and spilling his seed between us. "You are magnificent." He kisses my forehead while caressing me from my bottom to my shoulders.

I have never felt so adored.

"We should clean up and go back to the house," he whispers against my hair.

Deliciously sore, I rise and step into the cool water. A moment later, his arms are around me and nothing can be more perfect than floating in Oscar's arms while the sun gives its last moments of daylight.

I rise late, and while Oscar came to my bed and held me in the night, he is gone when I wake. Somehow that's disappointing, despite knowing he had no choice but to leave before the staff started their day.

Dressing, I'm delightfully sore and anxious to see him. We will finalize the details of the picnic today. Besides the fraudulent postings and the money taken, the books for Kensfield Manor are in good condition. I've made all the corrections and left notes for whoever takes the steward's job. That will be my last act as Oscar's Everton Lady. I will interview and hire a replacement to manage his estates.

Somehow that makes me very sad.

It's past eleven when I go downstairs.

Honoria is still at the breakfast table. "You're up late."

"I was tired." I sit next to her at the round table. It sits in an archway in front of windows that face west. The other seat is empty. "Did his lordship finish his breakfast already?"

Honoria sips her tea. "He was gone before I got up. I think he had an errand."

Trying not to look as disappointed as I feel isn't easy. I hope

I'm successful. "I see. Well, we'll finalize the menu for the picnic tomorrow without him."

"There will be some games, I'm told. His lordship hired a few circus performers. It should be good fun and the weather is so fine." Honoria grins like a girl.

"I'm sure it will be a fine time and perhaps will make up for the lack of a Lady Day celebration." I accept a cup of chocolate and spread butter on a piece of toast.

"Were the farmers satisfied with the financial agreement his lordship offered?" She finishes the last of her coddled eggs and puts her fork down.

A footman rushes over and takes the plate away.

We've been in Devonshire for several days and have accomplished so much that I'd nearly forgotten how brilliantly Oscar handled the seed situation. "They were pleased that his lordship explained all the details of what happened. He told them all the truth about Mr. Bellston, and he'll expect the cost of the grain to be deducted from what the farms pay this season."

"It's always wise to be honest." She sits back with her teacup. "I think he's in love with you, Ann."

My heart tightens as if someone has strapped a rope around it. "Who?"

"Don't be daft," Honoria scolds. "You know very well to whom I am referring.

Tears are trying very hard to push their way up as my emotions bubble. Joy, fear, and denial are all at odds inside me. I have to hold them at bay. "Oscar Stafford is not in love with me," I whisper, since a footman and Hodgins are still in the breakfast room.

"You don't think so?" Honoria smiles as if she has a secret.

I don't like it. "No. In fact, I'm certain you've lost your mind. Why would you say such a thing?"

Putting her cup in the saucer, she smiles, then pats her hair, which is already falling from its loose bun. "I believe it's obvious, my dear. He looks at you as if you are the sun and the moon. You can ask anyone who has seen the two of you together and they will say the same."

Like an imbecile, I look over at Hodgins.

The butler's stern expression softens, he gives a slight nod, and his expression returns to its natural state.

"I'm sure you're mistaken. Regardless, my work here is nearly done, and we will go back to London. I'm sure his lordship will travel to Scotland once there's a permanent steward in place." I should be stronger, but my chest aches with the idea that soon I'll never see Oscar again.

After three weeks at Kensfield, the books are in order and I've narrowed the search for a steward down to two gentlemen.

Oscar has been in good spirits, though we have not repeated our rendezvous at the pond. I know he goes there most nights, but I have stayed away. It's better this way. It would be foolish to become too attached to a man I cannot have. I made my choice years ago.

I check my hair in the glass. I'm to meet Oscar at the picnic and welcome the neighborhood.

Satisfied that my rose-colored dress is appropriate for the event, I feel good about the work I've done. As the day is lovely, I forgo a shawl and head downstairs.

Hodgins stands at the bottom of the stairs. "I was about to deliver this." He holds a letter. "It came for you a few minutes ago."

I take it and my heart sinks, immediately recognizing my name in my father's handwriting. "Thank you."

"Is something amiss, Miss Wittman?" He stares at me. "You've gone quite pale."

"It's nothing." I walk to the library and open the letter.

Ann,

I was more than a little surprised when a gentleman came to ask for your hand. I should have thought you long on the shelf. By my calculations, you are nearly thirty years of age. You probably regret your terrible decisions all those years ago and now wish you had listened to your father as any obedient daughter should do.

While my instinct was to tell the Earl of Kendall he was forbidden to marry you, he outranks me, and I gave my blessing. You should know that I believe you shouldn't marry an upstanding man. You have no right to such an elevated position in the ton.

Your mother is pleased for you. Perhaps that is enough.

Baronet, Niles Wittman

Gripping the paper in my fist, I walk out of the house to the lawn where people have already begun to assemble.

I scan the crowd. Local gentry in their bright colors mix with farmers in their Sunday best. Every table and tent is draped with pink and yellow fabric.

As festive as it all looks, my rage negates any pleasure.

Oscar stands at the center of everything, talking to the local magistrate. When he spots me, his expression brightens and falls in the span of an instant. He excuses himself and strides in my direction.

My bravado falters. I turn and walk as fast as I can toward the house. I don't know when I became such a coward, but it's time to go home. I'll pack and leave. It will be painless.

"Ann?" Oscar's raised voice is closer than I expect.

I stop just inside the garden's tall shrubs and face him. "My lord."

"What is wrong? You look as if you're... Actually, I've never seen you look this way. Are you angry?" He reaches for me.

I back away. The first tear finds its way to my cheek. "Don't think I'm crying because I'm sad. It is the rage that feeds my tears." I thrust the letter at him. "How dare you go to him."

He uncrumples the letter, looks at the page, and his jaw ticks. His eyes widen and his back stiffens. "I didn't realize."

The magistrate from the crowded lawn appears. "My lord, we cannot begin without you."

"Ann we will talk about this, but we have guests." He holds out his hand to me.

Tightening my fisted hands, I say, "No, my lord, you have guests. There is nothing to talk about."

Chapter Twelve

Oscar

More than an hour has passed by the time I can finally make my way back to the house. The foyer is empty, as is the rest of the house. Everyone is outside enjoying the day, a day that wouldn't have happened without Ann.

My hope to find her in the parlor or library is dashed, so I climb the stairs two at a time and go to her bedroom. I knock.

"I'm not feeling well. Go enjoy the party." There's a tightness in her voice that's out of character.

"May I come in, Ann?" I lean on the doorjamb with my heart in my throat.

She pulls the door open. "I don't want to see you. Go back to your guests." Her trunk is open in front of the bed and her dresses are spread out for packing.

"Are you leaving?" I fail to keep the panic from my voice.

She slumps into the chair by the fireplace. "I was always going to leave, my lord. I have left the names and credentials of the final two candidates for steward on your desk. You will meet with them next week and pick one. I'm sure you're anxious to get back to Scotland."

Oddly, that is not true. I like this house and the people in this area. The memories of my youth and my desire to be secluded kept me away. Now I see what I've been missing. However, if Ann is not here, then that may change. "I had no idea your father would write such a letter. I only wanted to do the right thing and to do it properly."

Head in her hand, she gazes at me. "My father has been finding fault in me all my life. The trouble, you see, is that I am not a man. Had I been born male, I'm sure he would have been a decent parent. As it was, I was flawed from the start and then dared to have a mind and will of my own."

My heart breaks for what she endured and my part in bringing that back to her. "I'm sorry. I only meant to get his permission as he is your father."

"It's of no real concern, my lord. I'll be leaving in the morning." She stands and returns to her packing.

"My name is Oscar." When she only nods, I say, "Then you are refusing to marry me."

The blue dress in her hands suffers as she fists the material. Slowly, she faces me. "As I was not consulted on the matter, I feel no regret in telling you that I will not marry you or anyone."

Pride stung, a string of unpleasant words come to mind. I hold my tongue. "Very well then, Miss Wittman. I thought after what we shared, you would be happy to receive a proposal. Clearly, I was mistaken. I apologize for being the cause of such a malicious letter from your father. That was certainly not my intention." I leave the room and close myself in the library while the picnic noise filters through the open windows.

Opening a bottle of brandy, I pour myself a glass and drink it in one gulp. How could I have been so mistaken about her feelings, when mine were so clear to me?

Bottle in one hand and glass in the other, I settle at my father's desk and pour another drink. Maybe I can forget how Ann Wittman felt in my arms and how her lips felt on mine. With enough brandy, I might even forget the enjoyment of being in her presence and solving problems together.

There are a few more bottles in the cellar. I may need to fortify my supply to reach that level of oblivion.

⸙

It's dark and the noise of revelry has subsided. The footsteps of staff going in and out of the house disturbed my drinking. With my head leaning on the arm of the settee, I turn it at the sound of the library door opening.

Honoria looks at me and the empty brandy bottle on the desk. She scans the open bottle on the table next to me. She crosses to the cart and takes a glass before sitting across the table and pouring herself a brandy. Sipping, she narrows her gaze. "What has happened? My maid tells me that Ann and I are to leave in the morning."

"She said she didn't want to marry me." I mean to pour another, but Honoria keeps the bottle near her, and I haven't the coordination l to get up and get it back.

"You proposed?" Those ever-watchful eyes of hers light up with excitement.

My chest tightens. "I never got the chance. She turned me down."

Nose scrunched, Honoria stares. "Forgive me, my lord, but I don't understand. If you didn't propose, how could she turn you down?"

"Her father beat me to it." I throw my hands up, but the abrupt action makes me dizzy and I lie still.

"Good lord, her father. Is that where you went the other day? You ask her father's permission to marry her? Why on earth would you do that?" It's the first time I've heard Honoria raise her voice.

With much effort, I try to shake off some of the fog in my head and sit up. "It's what a gentleman does when he wishes to wed a lady."

Her expression softens. "I imagine Ann was put out by you consulting her estranged father before her on the matter of her future."

"Furious." I cringe as I say it louder than I'd planned.

Honoria finishes her brandy and puts the glass and bottle down. "Listen to me very carefully. Clearly, you've pickled yourself because you're upset. However, you can still make this right."

"She ruined it. Well, I ruined it." I dig in my pocket. "I was going to propose today and give her this ring as a betrothal gift. I had it all planned for after the picnic. Now it's over." I drop the ring on the table.

There's a long silence. "Oscar?"

I look at her stern yet sympathetic face.

"Do you love Ann?" Her eyebrows rise and the candlelight makes her look like a ghost come to haunt me.

Letting my head fall back on the arm of the settee, it bangs hard. I rub the spot. "I think I loved her from the first moment I saw her at Everton House. Now, I love her so much, I don't know how I'm going to survive without her."

Honoria stands up and plucks the ring from the table. She hands it to me. "Tell her. I'm willing to bet, you didn't say all of that to her. If you had, my maid wouldn't be upstairs packing my trunk." She pats me on the head, and saunters from the library.

Staring at the ring, I know I need to do something, but my eyes are blurry. Once I'm on my feet, I make my way to the kitchen.

Cook is tidying the work table when she sees me. "Oh, it's like that, is it?"

"I need your help." I slump onto the chair against the wall.

She carries over a bucket. "First things first. Stick your finger down your throat and get what you can out of you. After that, we'll see what can be done."

When the sun comes up, I've had four hours of sleep and more water, tea, and ginger remedy than any man should have to endure. However, I'm coherent and nearly normal. Without waiting for my valet, I dress myself and go to Ann's room.

Empty except for her trunk waiting to be carried down to the carriage.

I nearly fall on my head running down the stairs, but catch the railing in time.

Perfectly beautiful at my father's desk, Ann stares at me.

I'm sure my running sounded like a herd of sheep had invaded the house. Attempting a smile despite the nerves and effects of excess alcohol roil in my stomach, I say, "I wonder if you would give me five minutes of your time. I know I don't deserve them, but please."

Eyes filled with unshed tears, she finishes writing something, puts the page aside, and stands. "I can't think of anything that needs saying."

"Please, Ann. I've made mistakes. I see that now. Just five minutes, I beg you." I don't know what I'll do if she refuses to hear me out. I suppose there will be nothing more I can do today.

"Say what you must." She crosses her arms over her chest and stares at some point over my shoulder.

Closing the door, I gather my courage. "I went to your father because I wanted to do everything right for you. I thought you desired his approval, and I thought this would gain you that. In hindsight, that was foolish and a bit naive. Had I realized the malice in his heart, I never would have subjected you to his rancor. I am more sorry than words can express."

Her jaw shifts from side to side and she glances at me before looking away. "I can see how that might have happened."

It's not exactly acceptance but I'll take it. "I had a stupid plan to gain his approval, then propose to you. I had it all planned for last night." I pull the ring from my pocket and hold it in my fist. Dropping to my knees, I watch as she looks at me. "I was going to get down on my knees and tell you how much I love you, how I've loved you since you walked into Lady Jane's office in London. I wanted you to know that you changed me and helped me to become the man I've always wanted to be. I don't want to hide away in Scotland and work on how to grow the best grain." I realize that's not entirely true. "Well, I do want to do those things, but that's not all I want."

She takes one step closer as her tears fall. "What other things do you want?"

"I'd like to be part of this community, attend the Lady Day celebration, and deliver the Christmas hams to the tenants. I'd like to go to balls, if you'll agree to dance with me. I'd like to marry you, have children, and do a better job of parenting than what you've known." My heart is going to pound out of my chest at any moment. I feel a bit sick and it has nothing to do with my stupidity from last night.

Closing the distance, Ann kneels in front of me. "If I did not love you so much that it aches in my soul, I should never forgive you for going to my father." She gasps for breath and more tears trail down her cheeks. "I never planned to marry. I never thought anyone would love me for more than a dowry."

Unable to stop myself, I thumb away her tears. "Your father already informed me there would be no dowry as that money was reallocated many years ago. Those were his words."

"I'm sure that's exactly what he said." She laughs. "I'm not young, Oscar. I'm a spinster. You're an earl. You could marry any one of the marriageable ladies out this year. They are beautiful and young. They have many years to give you a house full of children."

"You are beautiful inside and out, my Everton Lady. You are the only woman I will ever want. I love you so much that the pain of losing you was too much to bear. Can you forgive me?" I hold my breath.

"I do forgive you. I love you. It was like being struck by lightning the first time I saw you. I denied it even after we made love, but I'll not lie to myself anymore." She cups my cheek. "I love you and if you still wish it, I'll marry you, Oscar."

My heart surely can't take anymore. I drag her into my arms and kiss her hair, her forehead, anywhere I can reach. Finally, she turns her face, and I capture those plump delectable lips with mine.

Together, we generate fire and lightning. All I want to do is love Ann Wittman until the day I die. I may haunt her in the hereafter just to stay near her.

Breaking the kiss, I brush away the rest of the moisture

lingering on her cheeks. I take her hand and slide the sapphire and diamond ring onto her finger. "I'm determined to do something right. Ann, I love you more than anything or anyone. I promise to give you the life you deserve. Will you make me the happiest man alive and marry me?"

She brushes the hair from my forehead. "Oscar, I love you and I will marry you." She grins down at the ring. "This is lovely."

"You are lovely, the ring pales in comparison."

Cocking her head, she grins. "I had no idea you were a romantic poet as well as a scientist."

This slightly nauseous euphoria must be what happiness feels like. Her hand in mine, I stand, bringing her with me. "I think there are a great many things we still have to learn about one another, my love. I'm looking forward to every moment of education."

Epilogue

Ann

Being an Everton Lady was exciting and I loved almost every moment. However, being married to the man I love is ten times better. I don't even mind being the Countess of Kendall. Maybe I should reserve judgment for a few days at least, but I'm too happy to contain it.

"I hope you don't mind, that I invited your mother to our wedding breakfast." Oscar wraps his arms around me from behind and kisses my neck.

I hug his arms and breathe in the warm masculine scent of him. "I was surprised to see her at the ceremony. It was a delightful surprise. I'm glad you asked her to come and thrilled she consented. I saw her talking to Lord and Lady Everton. They seemed quite chummy. Even your mother looked happy."

Kissing me again where my neck meets my shoulder, he stirs longing inside me. "She seems genuinely happy for you, Ann."

"If you keep kissing me like that, we shall miss our own

wedding breakfast." My scolding falls short because his mouth is too distracting. "I only came up here to make sure my hair was still presentable and to catch my breath. You needn't have joined me."

With a last kiss, he takes my hand and leads me to the glass mirror and lady's dressing table newly installed in his room. Once I sit, he crouches to look at my reflection. "You are beautiful, perfectly so, my love."

I tuck one escaped curl back into the intricate weave of my hair. Honoria loaned me Margery for the occasion. "I suppose I'll have to hire a lady's maid of my own, now that I'm a countess."

His grin widens. "You forced my valet on me, so yes, you will need a maid."

With one last look at my appearance in smooth the bodice of my pale blue wedding gown. "I suppose we should go down and greet the guests."

Offering his hand, he bows.

I slip my fingers into his palm. We walk to the door of the room that we now share at Kensfield Manor. It's hard to keep worries from marring the day despite my happiness. The old memories of the home I grew up in, surface. "Will you promise me something?"

Hand on the doorknob, he stops and squeezes my fingers. "Anything."

"I don't want to be like my parents. Promise me, we'll always be the people we are today. My father rules my mother and he ruled me for most of my life." I slide my hand over my abdomen and meet his worried gaze. "When our child grows up, will you promise to let him or her make their own decisions?"

Dropping to his knees, he wraps his arms around me and

pulls me tight so his cheek is pressed to the place where our first child grows. "How long have you known?"

"I've suspected for a week. I'll have to see the doctor, but I'm reasonably certain that I'm with child." I run my fingers through his thick hair. "It's probably good since at my age, we haven't much time to build our family."

"We have the perfect amount of time, Ann. I would have made a terrible husband when I was younger. I hope to do the job justice now. I love you with all my being, heart, and soul. I will love our children; girls and boys alike. I promise to be a kind father who takes his children's wishes into account. However, I can't promise to deny a bad match for good reason."

I'm about to argue when he holds up his hand to slow my ire.

He stares at me from his knees, takes my hands, and kisses each in turn. "I promise that you and I will discuss these matters at length and together we will do our best for our children."

I lower to my knees despite the constraints of my corset and gown. "You are always telling me that I'm perfect, Oscar, but it is you who exceeds all my expectations with every moment we're together."

Someone scratches at the door. Hodgins speaks from the other side of the wood. "My lord, the guests are arriving."

Oscar helps me to my feet and presses his lips to my ear. "It will be my life's work to do so at every turn, my beautiful, kind, brilliant wife."

I dab the tear at the corner of my eye. Never having believed I deserved such a life, I pushed the expectations of my youth away, stuffing them deep inside. I thought them gone, but now they've come to the surface and brought all the joy of youth with them.

Smiling, Oscar skims his palm once more over my belly. "Are you ready?"

Afraid, words will bring me to tears with my emotions so close, I nod. Taking his arm, we face the rest of our lives together.

Thank you for reading *A Lady's Curves*.
I hope you enjoyed Ann and Oscar's story.
You can read more books about Everton Ladies in my series,
The Everton Domestic Society.

Get started with The Everton Domestic Society with
A Lady's Honor.
All the books can be read as stand-alone stories.

Also by A.S. Fenichel

HISTORICAL PARANORMAL ROMANCE

Witches of Windsor Series

Magic Touch

Magic Word

Pure Magic

The Demon Hunters Series

Ascension

Deception

Betrayal

Defiance

Vengeance

HISTORICAL ROMANCE

The Wallflowers of West Lane Series

The Earl Not Taken

Misleading A Duke

Capturing the Earl

Not Even For A Duke

The Everton Domestic Society Series

A Lady's Honor

A Lady's Escape

A Lady's Virtue

A Lady's Doubt

A Lady's Past

A Lady's Christmas

A Lady's Curves

The Forever Brides Series

Tainted Bride

Foolish Bride

Desperate Bride

Single Title Books

Wishing Game

Christmas Bliss

An Honorable Arrangement

CONTEMPORARY PARANORMAL EROTIC ROMANCE

The Psychic Mates Series

Kane's Bounty

Joshua's Mistake

Training Rain

The End of Days Series

Mayan Afterglow

Mayan Craving

Mayan Inferno

End of Days Trilogy

CONTEMPORARY EROTIC ROMANCE

Single Title Books

Alaskan Exposure

Revving Up the Holidays

WRITING AS ANDIE FENICHEL

Dad Bod Handyman (Lane Family)
Carnival Lane (Lane Family)
Lane to Fame (Lane Family)
Changing Lanes (Lane Family)
Heavy Petting (Lane Family)
Summer Lane (Lane Family)
Hero's Lane (Lane Family)
Icing It (Lane Family)
Mountain Lane (Lane Family)
Christmas Lane (Lane Family)
Texas Lane (Lane Family)
Building Lane (Lane Family)
Humbug Lane (Lane Family)
High Voltage Lane (Lane Family)
For Letter or Worse (Lane Family)
Dragon of My Dreams (Monster Between the Sheets)

Turnabout is Fairy Play (Monster Between the Sheets)
Soul of a Vampire (Brothers of Scrim Hall)
Soul of a Reaper (Brothers of Scrim Hall)
Soul of a Dragon (Brothers of Scrim Hall)
Soul of a Wolf (Brothers of Scrim Hall)
Soul of a Demon (Brothers of Scrim Hall)
Soul of a Phoenix (Brothers of Scrim Hall)
Soul of a Monster (Brothers of Scrim Hall)
Mantus
Riding With the Panther
The Manticore's Mate
Promised to the Satyr

**Visit A.S. Fenichel's website
for a complete and up-to-date list of all her books.
www.asfenichel.com**

About the Author

A.S. (Andie) Fenichel gave up a successful career in New York City to follow her husband to Texas and pursue her lifelong dream of being a professional writer. She's never looked back.

Andie adores writing stories filled with love, passion, desire, magic and maybe a little mayhem tossed in for good measure. Books have always been her perfect escape and she still relishes diving into one and staying up all night to finish a good story.

With over 55 published book, Andie Fenichel/A.S. Fenichel is multi-published in historical romance, paranormal romance, contemporary romance, and some interesting mixed genre romances too. Andie is the author of the several series, including Forever Brides, Everton Domestic Society, Witches of Windsor and more. Strong, empowered heroines from Regency London to modern-day New York are what you'll find in all her books.

A Jersey Girl at heart, she now makes her home in Southern Missouri with her real-life hero, her wonderful husband. When not reading or writing, she enjoys cooking, travel, history, puttering in her garden and spoiling her fussy cat.

Connect with Andie Fenichel
www.andiefenichel.com

Email: asfenichel@hotmail.com

facebook.com/a.s.fenichel
x.com/asfenichel
bookbub.com/authors/andie-fenichel
pinterest.com/asfenichel
tiktok.com/@asfenichel

Printed in Great Britain
by Amazon